The Shoemaker Prince

The Shoemaker Prince
2nd Edition
Copyright ©2023 by Jenny Prater

All rights reserved.
ISBN 978-1-952185-14-4

Printed in the United States of America
Published by Wax Heart Press, 2023
www.waxheartpress.com

For Grandpa Wally and Pam, for always supporting
me; I love you so much.

Table of Contents

The Girl With No Heart in Her Body.........................1
The Ogre Bride.........................7
The Shoemaker Prince.........................31
The Man Who Forgot How to Love.........................43
Windows.........................49
The Princess Who Refused to Marry a Merman.........................65
The Frog Who Married a Prince.........................77
The Foolish Princess and the Wise Prince.........................81
Flash.........................85
The Man With the Silver Nose.........................89
The Kiss and the Frog.........................95
King Lindorm.........................101
The Tailor and the Queen.........................107
Dreams Remembered.........................111
The Marquis of Carabas.........................115
Violet and Zorzal.........................121
Sources.........................179
Acknowledgements.........................181
Author's Note.........................183

The Girl With No Heart in Her Body

Long, long ago, in the days when dreams walked the earth, there lived a princess who was born with no heart in her body.

Naturally, this caused much consternation among the court. It was decided, after a week, that a ruby would be taken to fill the hole in her chest.

The child grew, as children often do, and she grew into a wicked, selfish thing, her stone heart unmoved by any diversion.

The days turned to months and the months turned to years, and it came time for the princess to be wed. Many men would love a heart of stone, but there were none that a stonehearted maiden could love.

And there came a prince with a quicksilver soul, who always heard yes when he should have heard no.

He contrived to be alone in the princess' bedchamber one night. She watched his coming with curiosity, for her heart was hardened to fear.

"Princess," he said, "What sits beneath your breast? For I have heard men call you heartless."

"I have a heart beneath my breast," she answered him, "and it shines brighter than yours, by far."

"Princess," he said, "I must see this heart. Surely you are not afraid to show it to me?"

"I am not afraid," the princess said, and she lifted her nightshirt up to her neck, to show the heart her parents had made her.

The prince forgot his lust for greed. He snatched the ruby from her chest, and stowed it in a pouch around his neck, and took himself quickly away.

The princess stared down at the hole in her chest for several minutes. Slowly, she dropped the hem of her nightshirt, and slowly, she put herself back to bed. No one had stolen her heart before. She did not know what to do.

In the morning, the princess found herself tired, and full of an unnamed sorrow, and she did not rise from her bed. Her parents worried, for their daughter was often up with the sun. But she would not rise, and she would not speak. She would not eat, and she would drink only a little water, and that only when her father begged, for every hour that passed took her heart farther from her body.

On the third day, the princess roused herself, and she went to her mother's jewel box, and tipped it over onto the floor.

The gold and silver she rejected immediately. She lingered over the jewels, sapphires and emeralds and diamonds. But all of these were wrong. She found a garnet broach, and thought, perhaps, perhaps. She found a pair of ruby earrings, and hope flared. But all of these were wrong.

Her heart was a stone the size of her fist. The earrings were each the size of a teardrop, and the garnet no bigger than her eyes, dry, for a girl with no heart could never cry.

The queen was not pleased to find her daughter had gone through her things. The queen was, in fact, altogether quite displeased with her daughter, and the king soon followed suit. For the princess would do nothing but lie abed all day, and refused to attend court functions, and refused to see any suitors.

And days turned to weeks, and weeks turned to months, and there came a dragon to lay waste at the north end of the kingdom.

"Perhaps," said the king to the queen, "we will marry her to the man who kills the dragon."

"Perhaps," said the queen to the king, "but what man would have a wife who lies in bed all day?"

"Perhaps," said the princess to herself, "the dragon has a jewel large enough to replace my heart."

And so the princess resolved to save herself from this wasting illness that no one else could see. At first she thought she would ride out to meet the dragon, but her body grew weaker and weaker as long as her ruby heart was gone, for no one could live forever without a heart.

She thought on this for many days, and at last she went back to her mother's room, and tipped over her jewel box again. She took from it as many things as she could carry, and then, giving up on her weak body, she filled the box again, and called a stable boy to carry it down, and tie it to the back of a large, reliable plow horse. She took herself slowly, next, down to the stables after the boy, and told him to tie her to the horse as well.

She pointed the horse's large, fuzzy nose to the north, and let herself rest, secure in the stable boy's knots. Her mother owned many, many fine pieces of jewelry, silver and gold and gems. If she was lucky, the princess thought, the dragon would smell the treasure, and come to meet her. She thought she could reason with a dragon; she still understood no fear.

The princess fell asleep on the back of the horse, and woke on the back of the horse, and drank a little from the skin of water the stable boy had filled for her. She slept again, and woke again, and so she passed many days, until the horse, plodding and reliable until now, suddenly reared up, dislodging princess and jewel box both, and galloped away.

She had reached the dragon's lair.

The princess stood slowly. She was bruised from the fall, and tired, always tired now, ever since the theft of her heart.

"Hello?" she called. "Is there a dragon here?"

There was no answer.

"I have brought many small treasures," she said, "which I would trade for one larger, if you are willing."

A long, red snout emerged from the cave before her, and she stumbled hastily back, for the breath from its nostrils was hot and painful.

The dragon sniffed her. The dragon sniffed the treasure. The dragon said, in a low, rumbling voice, "You are dying, little princess. Why have you come to me?"

"I have come that I might not die," the princess said. "My heart has been taken, and I would replace it from your hoard."

"I do not hoard the hearts of girls," the dragon said.

"I do not seek a heart of flesh," the princess answered. At this, the dragon picked her up, long yellowed teeth clamped gently about her waist, and pulled her into the cave. After a moment, it went back outside for the jewel box.

"This treasure is not yours, I think."

"It is my mother's. She will miss it far more than she will miss me, for I am a heartless, unloving child."

And the princess lifted her skirts up to her neck, and showed the dragon the hole in her chest. "Once I had a heart of stone," she said, "but it was stolen by a prince with a quicksilver soul, and without it I think I shall die. Nothing in the box is big enough to do."

She dropped her skirts and lifted her eyes, to see the shining jewels of the dragon's hoard. Light from the mouth of the cave bounced from each bright surface to the next, but the princess knew no greed, only hope.

"Will you help me?" she asked the dragon.

The dragon knelt to rest her snout above the hole where a heart should lie, and the heat of her warmed the empty chest. "I will help you," she said, and for the first time in her hard-hearted life, the princess knew joy.

"This evening I will find you a heart," said the dragon. "For now, little princess, you must rest." And she lifted the princess again, and laid her upon a sheep skin bed, and for the first time in her hard-hearted life, the princess knew peace.

When the princess woke, gems and jewels encircled her bed. "I have no red in my hoard," the dragon said, "but perhaps one of these will do."

They spent many days trying each jewel the dragon had, and when her hoard was finished, and a heart still not found, the dragon left the princess in her cave, and went out to discover new treasures. Days turned to weeks, and weeks turned to months, and each jewel took its turn in the princess' chest.

Diamond-hearted, she felt sharp, and harsh, and cruel. She said things she did not mean, and the dragon followed her with wide, wounded eyes. With silver in her chest, she felt an unending chill— all the blankets and skins the dragon had gathered could not keep out the cold, which settled deep in her bones.

With a giant pearl in place, she felt distant from all the world, and uncaring, too. She saw no problem until the dragon plucked it from her chest, and she returned to herself again. The opal made her giddy and prone to mood swings, wildly happy until she was suddenly sad. She kept it for several days, clinging to a joy she'd never known before, until the side effects became unbearable.

"Heart transplants are hard," the dragon said mournfully.

The princess patted her consolingly on the snout; the heart of gold had her feeling especially kind.

One night, as the princess slept with a rose quartz heart, a man crept into the cave. The princess woke as soon as he set foot inside, for rose quartz made her restless.

It was the quicksilver prince who had stolen her heart, and he wore it in a pouch tied about his neck. She could feel it from across the cave, fresh, as if it had just been ripped from her chest.

He carried a sword and a shield, as if he had come here to harm the dragon, her dragon, as he had harmed her. She reached beneath her dress and removed her rose quartz heart, for she wished to be herself at this meeting.

The moon emerged from behind a cloud, casting its light on the princess.

"Princess," said the prince. "I've come to save you."

"To save me," she repeated. "And what would you save me from?"

"From the dragon," he said. "Your parents are worried sick."

"Sick, are they? Sick as I was when you stole my heart? As I was when I languished for months without it?"

He smiled, eerie in the glittering light of the cave. "When the dragon is defeated," he told her, "I will give you my heart in return, and we will be wed before you father's throne."

The prince stepped forward, the princess stepped back, and the dragon raised her great head. "Who is this?" she asked, and the prince stepped hastily back again.

"This is the quicksilver prince who stole my heart. He has offered me his own in exchange."

"Oh?" said the dragon. "And how would you like it?"

"Charred," answered the princess, from the bottom of her lost stone heart. And the dragon opened her great mouth and breathed.

When the quicksilver prince was a pile of ash, and the princess's heart sat shining on top, she bent to pick it up, brushing off the soot. She lifted her dress and placed it inside her waiting chest.

The princess gathered her mother's jewels and the prince's steed, and she returned to her parents' palace.

"I am sorry I took your jewels," she said. "My heart has been not softened, but warmed, and I must go home to my friend. You need not send more princes after me."

Her parents did not understand, but parents often do not, and what they wanted, in the end, was to see their daughter happy. So she went back to her dragon, and lived happily there until the end of her days.

The Ogre Bride

The ogre had a daughter. The daughter was an ogre, too—which should, perhaps, have been expected, but young men seeking their fortunes had, in her experience, a baffling and infuriating expectation that ogre fathers would produce lovely human daughters.

She was quite fond of her father. He was a good man, insofar as he was a man at all. His one flaw, as far as she was concerned, was his desire that she be married.

It wasn't that she was opposed to marriage, in theory. It was just that there were no ogres on this side of the great sea who weren't family, quite old, or, usually, both, leaving only human men as potential husbands.

Her mother had been a human. This could, perhaps, have explained the expectation that she look human as well, had she gone about advertising her parentage to whomever she met. Which she did not.

Genetics were a funny thing. Her older brother looked exactly like a human man. He'd been a wonderful brother, until he'd married a princess with no idea he wasn't as human as her. He'd cut himself off from the family, then; she supposed he'd be back when his children began displaying the ogre-ish traits that often skipped a generation.

~

The ogre did not have a captive princess or a lovely human daughter who despised him. The ogre had a daughter who was also an ogre, whose name was Susan. His greatest desire was to see her wed, but alas, the young men who came to them, seeking their fortunes, were seldom interested in an ogre bride.

The ogre was the keeper of a vast estate with many gardens, and of the surrounding forest, which covered many leagues. It was through this forest that the various fortune seekers came.

He knew how it was, with fortune seekers. They wanted a task to complete, a mystery to solve, an enemy to fight. The ogre could provide all this, and it entertained him to do so. They liked it best if there was a maiden to win, as well, but he did not have an infinite supply of maidens lying about to hand out like candy to all the adventurers coming through. He had one daughter only, and few young men were worthy of her. None, in fact, that he had met thus far.

Most of the fortune seekers were kept to the forest, to complete their tasks there; the ogre made a few small appearances throughout their quests, and allowed them to make off, in the end, with some small amount of treasure, insignificant to him. Only the likelier candidates for Susan's hand made it as far as the gardens. They would come close enough to see the manor, perhaps, but none had yet earned the right to enter.

None should have met Susan, either, but she had a habit of sneaking out to introduce herself. She helped them, sometimes, with their tasks, or tried to—they often refused her help. He thought she enjoyed the challenge of the tasks more than meeting the young men, and often enlisted her help to test a new task before setting it for their fortune seekers.

Their life was a simple one, despite the size of their estate, consisting of long, happy days filled with gardening and fishing and designing new puzzles. Someday Susan would marry, and he would be alone again, at least until his son inevitably returned home, or sent his children home, when their genealogy became obvious to his wife. For now, though, it was Susan and the ogre, their idyllic days interrupted occasionally by young men too foolish to want her.

~

It was in the spring of her twenty eighth year that the knight came. He was not the first knight to seek his fortune there. But he was the first who mattered.

He had the same warm, dark skin as Susan's dead mother and lost brother, and a face that always smiled, and a dappled mare which he called Felicity.

Susan watched his progress through the forest—she often did this when she was bored, through the enchanted telescope her father had given her on her fourteenth birthday. He made it through the forest, and all its usual challenges, far more quickly than expected, and by the time he reached the clearing where their home and gardens laid, Susan's father was still at the opposite end of the forest, playing the villain for some other young fortune seeker.

Susan sighed. They weren't supposed to pass the forest until Father had deemed them worthy-ish, and none had managed to do so before. They couldn't be allowed to wander about unattended, once they'd made it this far; she would have to go out and greet him. She didn't like to be the one to make first contact. It was meant to be an intimidating experience, for the fortune seeker, and she'd never intimidated well. Except for by accident, which was largely just humiliating.

"Good evening," she said when she reached him. She'd never practiced the kind of alarming greetings her father excelled at, and didn't want to embarrass herself improvising.

"Hello," he said. "I was told there dwelt a maiden here, seeking rescue from an ogre."

She sighed. This rumor made its way through the surrounding kingdoms with irritating frequency—she suspected her father of starting it to lure in more potential suitors for her.

"I'm afraid you've been misinformed," she told the knight. "I am the only maiden here, and the ogre is my father."

"And your father treats you well?" the knight asked.

"He does," Susan said, surprised. A fortune seeker had never asked such a question before. And usually they would not take her word for it, when she told them there was no one here in need of rescue.

"I am sorry for disturbing you, then. Is there any assistance I might provide, as long as I'm here?"

This, at least, was familiar territory, though usually they didn't offer to help—usually her father demanded their help before allowing them to leave. It was all part of the fortune seeking game.

"My father will return in the morning, and he will set you three tasks. You may sleep in the stable with your horse tonight."

She went back into the house, trusting him to find his own way to the stable—she wasn't often trusting, with fortune seekers, but she had a good feeling about this one. She sifted through her father's list of impossible tasks before bed, trying to think which ones would suit him best.

~

The ogre returned from the forest just after dawn, and went to wake his new guest as soon as Susan had told him the story.

The man scrambled up as soon as he let the stable door slam closed—he was disheveled from the night sharing a stall with his horse, but did not seem overly concerned at the appearance of an ogre.

"Hello, sir. My name is Roland. I should have—I'm sorry, it was rude of me—I forgot to introduce myself to your daughter last night. Thank you very much for your hospitality; it's the nicest stable I've slept in."

He seemed earnest, and sincere. They hadn't had one of those in a while. It had been a long rash of entitled little brats, these last few years, and a higher rate than usual of task failure. It helped, the ogre suspected, that this one seemed to be only a knight, not a prince. And a few years older than their usual visitors.

Well, he didn't seem to be intimidated, and was behaving politely enough; there was no need to put on a show, then. Not yet—he'd see how things progressed.

"You came to free a captive maiden?" he asked.

"No, sir. I mean—well, yes, but only incidentally. I am sorry—you see, they told me, in the village, that there was one, and I thought I'd best look into it, as long as I was here."

"What did you come for, then?"

"There is a little prince in my land who was born ill. It is not an urgent matter, exactly, but the doctors say he will likely not live to adulthood. I would—I would like to find a cure for him. He is a good, sweet boy, and the only child of the king and queen. The cousin who will inherit if my prince dies is a wicked man, and he— I have searched far and wide for a cure. I have been away from my home for over a year, now. I think you are my last chance."

Sicknesses were tricky. It was always better when they came seeking treasure, which he could provide, or brides, which he couldn't. Best was when all they really wanted was some sense of personal validation. The maybes were just so difficult. He hated to give false hope, especially to nice young men like this one. Especially when he was seeking to save an innocent child.

"I will see what I can do. Tell me everything you can about the illness. Then, while I research, perhaps you could help me with some chores."

The man nodded. "Certainly, sir. I'd be happy to help."

Oh, he liked this one. He did hope he could find a cure.

~

Susan didn't wait long in the morning to go looking for the knight. Roland, her father had called him. It was important he succeed in his tasks, when the reward he sought was a child's health. And he seemed the sort of man who would allow her to help.

He was not, as it turned out. She found him with the grains to organize—a common first task.

"I could help you," she offered, as she often did at this stage. She was more surprised than usual when he shook his head.

"I wouldn't want you to get in trouble with your father," he said.

Well. That was an unexpected development, and a tricky one. Some tasks could really only be completed by accepting help. But usually men refused her help because she was a disgusting ogre. She'd never had one refuse in the interest of protecting her family relationships, and didn't know what to do about it—it hardly seemed fair that he could fail a task because he was a nice young man. This wasn't one of the tasks that absolutely required her assistance, but it was likely he would have one later on.

"You're to use whatever resources you have available to complete the task," she said after some consideration. "And I'm making myself available to you today."

He frowned. "It seems like cheating."

"Would you risk your little prince's life for your own sense of honor and pride?"

"No," he said. "I would not."

"Do you know how you'll accomplish the task?"

"I've just begun to think on it. I haven't an idea yet, but I should like to think a little more, if you don't mind, before accepting defeat and assistance."

"Very well," she said. "I shall bring you lunch in a few hours, and we will discuss it further then."

He thanked her for lunch, when she returned—they didn't usually thank her—and said, "I think you are right that I cannot do this alone. But I should not like to pit you against your father. If any resources are allowed, there are others I could call for help, if you do not mind."

Susan did not mind. She thought it quite sweet, his worry about her and her father. When lunch was finished, she sat and watched as he summoned a hundred thousand ants, who made short work of the grain.

He was one of those, then—they were always the type her father thought made likely suitors. Men who had been kind to creatures they met in the woods, and the creatures would come to help them later in their quests. Usually, those men were kind to animals, but not to ogres. And they snuck about, trying to hide their helpers from Susan and her father. She'd never been asked permission to summon the ants, before.

She'd never watched them work, up close, though she'd seen it in her telescope. Ants or birds were helpful here, occasionally other small animals. It was different, up close. The ants lingered. Roland introduced her to them as "My new friend Susan," and seemed to know several by name. Not nearly all, of course—ultimately an insignificant amount, when there were so many. But he named them to her as he could, Lifter-of-Rocks and Three-Green-Leaves, Father-of-Many and Queen-Who-Will-Be, Far-Traveller and One-Who-Wanders-Deep-Tunnels. They crawled over her hands and feet, and she laughed at the tickling feeling of them.

"You have done well," she told him when the ants were gone. "I will tell my father you have finished, and he will come to see."

"Thank you," Roland said. "Do you—do you think he will find the cure for my prince?"

"He will do his best," Susan said, for that was as much a promise as she could make. "And I will help him."

The next day Roland was set his second task, which was to drain the small, scummy pond at the east end of the estate, with no supplies offered but a sieve.

"Am I permitted to enlist help, again?" he asked when Susan came to check his progress.

"You are always permitted to ask for help. Being kind enough to others that they are willing to help is how you prove your worthiness."

"Oh. I see. Do you know—it's a small pond, unconnected to any other water. Does it have any fish in it?"

"I think so, though not as many as it used to. That's partly why Father wants it drained; the scum has killed off so much of it he decided we'd best just start over."

"I think—if there are any fish at all in the pond, I think I have a solution. But is there another body of water nearby? I wouldn't want to ask fish for help, and then see them die of it."

"There's a river a quarter mile from here."

"Would it be all right if I asked you for a bucket? I know I can't use it to drain the pond, and of course you can watch me to be sure I don't. But I'll have to move the fish quickly, when the pond is drained, and I don't think a sieve is well suited to the task."

"I can get you a bucket," Susan said, and the request gave her a warm, fluttery feeling. She'd seen many young men enlist fish to help empty ponds. Men who had earned the help of those fish by being kind to them, early in their journeys. Men who, as far as she could see, left those fish to flounder and die in the ponds they'd emptied—so much, then, for their kindness to fish.

She went and fetched not a bucket, but a trough full of fresh, clean water, and loaded it into a cart. By the time she brought the cart to the pond, it was more than half drained, and seemed to contain nearly as much fish as it did water. She began lifting fish out of the pond and into the trough, and Roland began to help her, as the pond continued to shrink. Finally there was only one small fish sitting in the mud, and Roland lifted it gently, thanking it as he did so.

"To the river, then," Susan said, lifting the handles of the cart.

"Let me, please," Roland said.

"I'm quite certain I'm stronger than you."

"Perhaps, but this is still part of my task, and I would not feel right making you do the work, when I am perfectly capable of doing it myself."

She let him take the handles, and did not tell him that this was not part of his task—that others had left the fish to die, and that sometimes she had saved them herself, and other times she had quickly killed them all and made them into dinner.

~

"Can we cure his prince?" Susan asked her father that night.

"We can, but it will lengthen his trials a little—there are ingredients to be gathered."

"I can help him."

The ogre smiled. "You're quite taken with this one, aren't you?"

"I am," she admitted.

"Good. I believe he likes you as well."

~

On the third morning, she found Roland in one of the little bits of forest they needed cleared for a new garden. Father had given him an axe made of glass. That was one of her favorite challenges—she thought it was ever so much more fun than the axe with no blade. There was no functional difference, of course, but it was little details like this that made their estate such a popular destination for fortune seekers.

"This is the final task that will give you access to the cure," she told him, "but it is only a recipe. You will have to find the ingredients, still. Will you let me help you?"

"If you would like to."

"And with the forest, as well?"

He glanced around at the trees. "It is true that I do not have a pack of friendly lumberjacks at my beck and call. You are sure your father will not mind?"

"He will not mind. But I must wait until you fall asleep—those are the rules."

Roland nodded. "It would seem, then, that we have a few hours to fill, as I do not plan to sleep so soon after waking. Perhaps you would like to explore a bit of the forest, with Felicity and myself?"

"I would like that very much. I will prepare a picnic, while you prepare your horse, and meet you back here shortly."

~

That night, when Roland slept in the stable with Felicity, Susan took the glass axe, which was also an enchanted axe, back to the bit of forest in need of clearing, and spoke the words that made it work. And in the morning, Susan's father gave Roland the recipe that would heal his prince, and in the afternoon, Susan and Roland set out with Felicity to find its ingredients.

Some of the things they needed must be tracked down and dug up out of the ground, and at this, Roland excelled. But it was good that Susan was there, for it saved him completing many more impossible tasks. The old woman who lived in the house with chicken legs, the little gnome who lived in the log, the lady who dwelt underground, the talking bear who had once been a prince before he decided he preferred life enchanted—they, too, were all setters of impossible tasks for fortune seekers. But they were also Susan's aunts and uncles, her childhood babysitters, and because she was there, and because she asked, they gave Roland what he needed without making a game of it.

When they went down the well to the underground home of Susan's Auntie Angharad, she said to Roland, "You may have the roots, but only if you promise to marry our Susan."

"Yes," said the bear prince, who was visiting, "then you may have my berries, too."

Susan sighed. She knew she should have left Roland above, and come to see Auntie Angharad alone.

"I—I haven't even asked yet if she would like to marry me," Roland objected.

Yet, Susan thought. He hadn't asked her yet—that meant he did intend to.

"You'd best get to it, then," advised the bear. Which was how Susan and Roland came to be betrothed.

~

"I must take the cure home," Roland said, "and then I will come back to you."

"You want to come back here?" asked Susan, who had always imagined she would have to move to some far-off land, if ever she did get married.

Roland blushed. "I—that is, if you and your father don't mind? I know that you are fond of each other, and that he is a good man, and that you are settled here; I do not get on with my parents, and have spent most of my adulthood travelling, and there is nothing there for me to inherit and share with you, as I am the fourth son."

Susan nodded. She had not wanted to leave her father, really, and knew her father had not looked forward to losing her, either. "How long will it take you, to get there and back?"

"I imagine it will be about five months one way, on Felicity, without the many stops I made on the way here. I do—I live very far away. And I imagine I will need to stay a few weeks, to see that the prince is healed properly, and to say my goodbyes, and get my things in order."

"Nearly a year, then."

"I hope—I will understand, if you do not wish to wait so long."

"It's not as if I have other suitors waiting in the wings, Roland. I've waited my whole life for you—what's a year more?"

~

Eleven months passed, and Susan filled her time as she usually did, helping her father and watching the fortune seekers and visiting friends in the forest. Soon, she thought, at the eleven-month mark, soon he would be back. Allowing ten months for a round-trip journey, eleven left him a whole month to get his affairs in order.

Eleven months and one week, then eleven months and two. At eleven months and eighteen days, her determination broke, and she turned to her enchanted telescope to find him.

The telescope could not find people by name—the only enchantment on it was that it could see farther and clearer than any other, and through walls. It was still up to her to point it in the right direction. But surely, surely, by now he would be close enough that he would not be too hard to find.

He was very difficult to find. She started in the early morning, and by the late evening there was no sign of him. She had searched the entire forest in the direction he should have come from, and there was nothing—how could he not even have entered the forest yet?

Perhaps he had been delayed at home. She searched farther afield, moving the telescope slowly and carefully, looking for the small shape of a dark man on a light horse. She searched through leagues and leagues and leagues, constantly afraid that she had missed him, and finally fell asleep with no more answers than she'd had that morning.

It was late the following afternoon that her telescope reached a land where all the people had clothes cut like his. He could not— surely, he could not be still at home. Unless there had been some accident—what if he had died on the road, and had never made it home at all?

She found the capital city, and the palace, and inside of it a happy, healthy little boy with a crown sitting crooked on his head.

Roland had made it home, then. He'd healed his prince.

She searched through the rest of the city. There were signs of a celebration—a wedding, she realized slowly. A wedding coming. It was when she caught site of a bulletin on the ground that she truly—

The wedding of Sir Roland, it said. In eight days' time. It—he couldn't. He wouldn't. Not Roland.

She searched more frantically, but the telescope was not enchanted to compete with darkness falling, and she still had not found him when it was too dark to see.

She began to search immediately again in the morning, and this time she found him quickly. He was in a building which must have been his home—everything was a flurry of activity and wedding preparation, but he was not in the midst of it. He was in a small room alone, sitting on the bed, and the door was closed.

He looked—wrong. He did not look like a man preparing for a wedding. He was much thinner than he had been when she saw him last, and his hair was less well kept—though she thought a man at home should be able to care for himself better than one on the road for months on end.

She focused the telescope more—it was a very powerful telescope—and saw that his eyes were glassy and strange. The door—there were dents and gouges in the wood around it, as if someone had tried to force his way out.

Something was very wrong. Susan ran to find her father.

~

"Something is wrong," the ogre agreed. "We must get you to him, and quickly."

"It took him five months by horse, and the wedding is in seven days. I would never make it in time."

The ogre was silent for a time, thinking. "The seven league boots," he said at last. "If you leave tomorrow morning, in those, you'll reach him by that night, with plenty of time to solve the problem."

~

She left the following dawn. She packed lightly, only a bit of fruit from the orchard, and a bit of dried meat, to eat throughout the day, and enough for a few days more, in case. And the cloak of invisibility, which her father insisted on, for safety. It could be dangerous, being an ogre in civilized lands. She and Roland would be home very quickly if all went as planned. The boots could be tricky, with more than one person, but he seemed to have lost so much weight, and she was an ogre—she could likely carry him, and move just as quickly as ever in the boots. Or they could hold hands, and take one boot each—each step would take them three and a half leagues, then.

Oh, but there was Felicity. He would want to bring her along, and that could be tricky. She added a bit more food to her pack. It may have been a bit past its prime, some of it, but she didn't have time to worry about that.

She was in a hurry, but there was one stop she would allow herself to make.

She paused in a place they called land of the Thunder Prince, for her brother had earned a name for himself when he went out to seek his fortune.

It was foolish to stop here. Thunder-and-Lightning would not want to see her. He had been playing at being human for half her life now. She doubted he even went by that name anymore—his name was as ogre-ish as hers was human, a deal made between their parents many years ago. Thunder Prince was a title; she didn't know what name he might use now.

The city was in chaos when she arrived, and she stayed beneath her invisible cloak, listening. There was some disagreement, it seemed, as to whether the princess had been cursed, or had been unfaithful to her husband. For she had given birth last night to a monster.

Damn it, Thunder.

She untied the laces on her boots, to turn off their magic, and let herself into the palace, which made their estate look like a hovel—it took her an hour to follow the shouting to a bedchamber, where she found her brother, a lovely blonde princess, and a bassinet.

"I'm finished," the princess was saying as Susan slipped into the room. "Take the little beast and get out of my kingdom, before someone burns at the stake over this debacle."

She stormed out of the room, slamming the door, and Susan slipped off her cloak.

"Susan?"

"Hello, Thunder. Show me the baby?"

He gestured toward the bassinet. He looked old, and tired. Susan ignored him. It was only fair; he'd ignored her for fifteen years now.

"Hello, darling," she murmured, bending over the bassinet. It was a beautiful little girl, with an ogre-ish face and soft, human skin, red and new. It wasn't until she lifted the baby into her arms that she noticed the legs, burning and blistered and wrong.

"What happened?"

Thunder sighed. "Its mother threw it into the fire when she saw what it was."

"It?" Susan repeated. Thunder must have pulled her back out of the fire, at least.

He shrugged, looking uncomfortable.

"Back home to Father, then?"

"I suppose so."

"You can take the seven league boots," she offered recklessly. "I can finish my journey at a standard pace. Father will want to meet his granddaughter as soon as possible."

Thunder scowled. "I'm not taking that thing with me. It ruined everything."

"This thing is your daughter, Thunder. Your daughter, who your wife just tried to murder."

"I don't want it. I'll take the others, though."

"The others?"

"It's our third child. The first two were human passing."

Susan took a moment to consider her options. An innocent, injured infant was obviously the most important thing. But Thunder was her brother, even if he was being a colossal idiot. She could care for a baby. She couldn't make her brother a better person. But maybe someone else could. And if there were two other children to consider—human passing didn't mean human. They were as ogre as their baby sister, and recent history indicated their mother would kill them for it, if it showed someday. She slipped off her boots.

"Get the other children and go home. Father will straighten you out. I wouldn't trust you to travel home with the baby at this point, anyway, and I don't have time to go back myself."

She swept herself and the baby beneath the cloak, not bothering with a goodbye—Thunder didn't deserve it.

It was a shame, giving up the boots. But she still had her cloak, and the sooner Thunder was home, the better. Father would straighten him out—he had to. And the other children couldn't stay here, of course, but if Thunder cared so little for his newest baby— she would have to trust him to keep them safe for the distance of the journey, which would not be long. But she did not want the man he had become to be solely responsible for any children for the weeks the trip would take with standard shoes. The three of them had to return to Father as soon as possible, and the boots were the best way to do that.

As for her journey—it was five months by horse. That came to a hundred and fifty days. How much more quickly, she wondered, did a horse travel than a man? Each step in the seven league boots was equal to a day's journey in standard shoes.

She had taken one hundred and ninety three steps before finding Thunder and her niece. Surely, that must bring her close.

But if Roland was truly to wed another in six days—

It had been foolish, giving the boots to Thunder. She had wanted him out of her sight. She had wanted him and the other children still alive. But each step was worth seven hours of walking, and she doubted she could walk much more than seven hours in a day, especially with an infant. Even if she had been only eight or nine steps away, before, she would never make it in time.

There was no help for it now. She turned her attention to the child that was now her responsibility.

One quarter ogre. Was that enough to make Susan qualified to care for her? Ogre infants needn't breastfeed, though it was beneficial if they did. The baby was asleep, then; Susan slid a finger carefully into her mouth.

Teeth. Good. That much an ogre, then—enough to make things easier. Though not by much. She had six days to travel an uncertain distance with a newborn, mostly human child in tow.

Thunder had come to this land, initially, to seek his own fortune. That meant there must be someone like her father nearby.

Susan would seek her fortune. Hopefully her fortune would look like a diaper bag and fast transportation.

The baby's wounds, at least, weren't nearly so bad as they would be for a full human. Though a full human wouldn't have sustained these wounds in the first place—that was the whole problem. It was impossible to tell, at this stage, whether the function of the legs had been damaged—she wouldn't begin using them for months.

There had been a sticky, ointment smell to the baby when Susan first picked her up, and she'd had the forethought, at least, to follow that scent to a small glass jar, and bring the jar with her when she left the palace. Someone had cared enough to get a burn cream for an ogre child, and she was horribly afraid it had not been the child's half ogre father. Certainly, it was not his wife.

Susan made her underskirt into a sling—the baby woke, and cried, when placed inside—and dug through her pack for a bit of apple, just beginning to rot, just enough to make it soft enough for a set of baby teeth. The baby sucked on it, quieting slowly.

That left her with one major issue for the baby—a name. It was not safe for children to be out in the world without a name. If her parents had bothered to name her, it would not have been given with love, which would render it as worthless as no name at all.

"Wind-and-Sea," she said aloud, "daughter of Thunder-and-Lightning." That would do. A proper ogre name was best, for a child rejected by humanity. Susan's human name had been a gift from her human mother—Wind-and-Sea's mother had given her only scars and possible nerve damage.

Child fed. Child named. Time, then, for Susan to seek a fortune.

~

It was at midday the next day that she found what she was searching for—a fearsome-looking, elderly ogre who would set her three impossible tasks. They would begin, he told her, early the following morning.

"Oh, mightn't I start now? I'm in a terrible hurry."

"At dawn," the old ogre repeated, and walked away.

She slept fitfully, and so did the baby, whose burnt little legs must surely ache terribly, even with all the ointment applied. Susan thought her father would have allowed better accommodations, and more haste, for a fortune seeker carrying an injured child. She had been told to sleep behind the stable, not even inside.

It was late morning by the time the ogre returned, and Susan had been up for hours, pacing and worried, feeding Wind-and-Sea bits of fruit and trying to sooth her.

There was a great speech to be given before she could begin, but that was standard enough. "And if you fail any task," the ogre finished his spiel, "you will die."

Oh. Well, that seemed—but part of her father's role in this game was to frighten—surely that was all this was.

Her first task was to sort chaff and load in into great sacks, which was familiar territory, at least. She counted out the sacks, to see how much work there was—twenty.

There was a magic to this, at home, but the same words would not work for a different sorcerer's task. There were a few courses she could take, but she was in a great hurry, and had a child to mind, besides.

"Lifter-of-Rocks," she called, quietly. "Far-Traveller, Three-Green-Leaves." She did not know if they would come for her—she had showed them no kindness in the woods. But Roland had introduced her as a friend, and she had their names, which were power. "Roland is in trouble, and I need your help to save him."

It was not many minutes before a great host of ants appeared, and they worked quickly as she explained the situation. Before long there were four bags filled, but the pile of chaff to be sorted looked no smaller, though nearly a quarter should have been gone.

With a horrible feeling in her stomach, Susan went to count the empty sacks again. Still twenty. The ants filled one more, and the count remained the same.

Oh. Oh, no. "You will die," he had said. This ogre was nothing at all like her father, who wanted his fortune seekers to succeed, who gave them every chance, and only sent them home empty-handed when they failed. This task was truly impossible. A trap.

She thanked the ants and sent them on their way, quickly, and ran deep, deep into the woods. She could not be taking any chances, with a baby strapped to her chest.

It was likely the evil ogre would chase her. But Susan's father was a sorcerer of some significance, and her natural magic would likely work to hide her. Besides, there was the cloak of invisibility. The magic to see beyond that must be very strong.

There wasn't time for this! Roland's wedding was so soon, and she was still so far away.

~

She walked as quickly as she could for the next few days, sleeping seldom, giving most of her packed food to the baby. She had money, but these were human lands, and an ogre could not simply walk into town and purchase a horse and a meal. Ogres were to be killed on sight, in many places.

There was the cloak. But the cloak would not hide the sounds of an increasingly unhappy infant—oh, why had she given up the boots, and kept the baby? Why did Thunder have to be so difficult?

And even without the baby—she could steal food, perhaps, while invisible, or even take it and leave money behind. But making off with an entire horse—besides, a horse would not be nearly fast enough. The wedding—she counted the days, and counted them again, just to be sure.

The wedding was this evening. At sunset, the bulletin she saw had said, and it was already midmorning. She could not—she could not possibly make it in time. But she could not give up. And she could not turn around and go home, either. However would she make it that far, on foot, and with the baby?

Her father would come for her. He had the boots back, now, and he could find her. But that was only assuming that Thunder had actually returned home, and not torn off on some other foolish adventure. And assuming that her father even knew where to find her. She had become turned around, a bit, when she tried to seek her fortune, and she was only mostly sure that she was still going in the correct direction. He couldn't seek her out with the telescope, first—she was wearing the cloak. And even if she hadn't been, the telescope was attuned to her, specifically. Which had seemed magnificent when she was fourteen and full of small, secret thoughts, but seemed very foolish now, when her father couldn't use it to bring her home.

She should take off the cloak, to increase his chances of finding her by other means. But she was still in so populated an area, and still so obviously an ogre.

It was mid-afternoon when she finally, finally had the stroke of luck she'd been longing for since she first reunited with her brother.

She'd been walking through the woods for an hour or more, singing herself hoarse with lullabies, when she reached a clearing where two giants were arguing over a pile of enchanted items. She stopped her singing and hushed Wind-and-Sea as best she could, taking a few minutes to watch them and consider her options. She didn't even know, yet, if the giants had anything that would help her. But if they did, would they lend or sell it to her? Or would they be cruel, like Thunder's wife, and the old ogre, and all the fortune seekers who'd come before Roland?

They were fighting over who each item belonged to, and as she was watching a young man approached, from the opposite direction, and offered to help them settle the argument.

The giants agreed, and described each item to the man. One was a saddle, to ride the wind.

It was not a windy day. Catching a ride on a breeze would not be of much use, now. But if one saddled the wind, then one could command it, make it go faster.

The young man tested out one of the other items, and Susan listened as the giants, a few steps away, planned quietly to kill and eat him when their score was settled. No reason, then, to feel bad for stealing from them. She checked that her cloak was fastened, and the baby strapped tight to her chest, and rushed forward to grab the saddle.

~

There was nothing in the world like riding the wind. Susan turned her stirrupped heels inward, urging it faster and faster, as Wind-and-Sea shrieked with laughter. By the time they reached the seaside city she'd seen in her telescope, the sun was just touching the horizon. She delighted in blowing the wedding banners all away as she landed. She was in time. She would find out what had happened and fix it, before Roland married another.

The saddle was a little unwieldy, but there was no help for that. She could hardly leave it lying about, so she tucked it under her cloak as best she could, and made her way into the hall where the wedding was to take place.

There was a great crowd of men and women in what she imagined were their finest clothes—Susan had little experience with fine clothing, herself, most of the people she met being in the midst of long and dangerous journeys.

At the center of it all was Roland, standing between a beautiful human woman and an older couple who she thought might be his parents. And seeing him with her telescope was nothing at all like seeing him with her eyes.

He looked horribly ill. He was pale, his hair limp and lifeless, and his expression was confused and far away. When she came very close, still invisible, she could see that he was shaking.

Never mind, even, that he was supposed to be marrying her— who would think to have a wedding at all for a man who was so obviously not well?

The priest had begun to speak, already, and Susan threw off her cloak.

She was an ogre woman in a crowd of humans—elegant, well-dressed, mostly armed humans, and she was a bedraggled ogre woman in travel-worn clothing, a baby strapped to her chest with her undergarments, dragging an empty saddle behind her.

The room fell silent.

"Susan?"

Roland stepped toward her, his face clearing a little, and the people she thought were his parents grabbed him, tried to hold him back. He pulled away from them and stepped forward again, stumbling; Susan caught him as best she could, mindful of the child on her chest.

"Susan," he said, and his voice was hoarse and frantic. "Susan, we have to leave, now."

She swept the cloak around them both and set the saddle on the ground, sitting on it and pulling him down into her lap. As soon as she turned in her heels they were off, and they rode the wind until they were too far away to be followed.

Susan stopped in a clearing by a stream, and as soon as they were back on the ground, Roland stumbled away, throwing up until there could be nothing left inside him, and then heaving for a minute more. She waited, with a hand on his shoulder, until he was done; the ride had not made her nauseous, but he had been unwell already.

"Come get some water," she suggested when he seemed finished, and he nodded shakily.

They drank, and sat together at the bank of the stream, and Susan fished one of the last bits of fruit from her pack to feed Wind-and-Sea. She studied Roland's face; his eyes seemed a little clearer, at least.

They sat in silence for some time before he said quietly, "They've been drugging me. I don't—I don't know how long, now. I'm only a fourth son; they've never bothered much about me. But when I cured the prince, they thought I could make a better match than my brothers. They were angry enough, when I told them I was engaged, but I let slip, somehow, that you were an ogre, and they— they decided you must have enchanted me, and they've been trying to 'break the spell,' mostly by holding me down and pouring nasty things down my throat."

"I'm sorry. I should have come looking for you sooner."

He shook his head. "I don't—you had no way of knowing. I don't even know how long it's been—so many things have become rather a blur. I think—I think I threw up the last bit of whatever poison they've been using, but I'm sure there's still more in my system."

"I'll take you home," she said, "and it will be all right. Only—Felicity. We could go back for her, but I don't know how she'd do, riding the wind, and we can't take the long way—I don't have any supplies left, really, and you're not well."

He shook his head again. "She's dead. My father killed her. They tried—they tried to scare me straight, before they resorted to drugging me."

"I'm sorry."

They both fell silent again, Roland resting his head on her shoulder. She straightened, eventually, and fished the last bit of dried meat from the bottom of her pack. Wind-and-Sea fussed.

"Do you think you could eat a little?" Susan asked.

"Not yet," Roland said. "I don't—I know my memory isn't all right, at the moment, but a baby—we didn't—"

"No, we didn't. She's my niece. I rescued her on my way here." Susan lifted her out of the sling, careful not to bump her blistered little legs, and set her on her lap. Roland, she thought, was too shaky still to hold a baby.

"Wind-and-Sea," she said, "this is Roland, who will be your uncle. Roland, this is Wind-and-Sea, daughter of Thunder-and-Lightning. Her mother threw her into the fire when she saw she was an ogre. My brother and his older children have gone home to my father, I hope, but I kept her with me, because Thunder was being an ass."

"She's beautiful," Roland said softly.

Susan nodded. "Would you like to go home?"

"Very much," Roland said. She strapped Wind-and-Sea back in against her chest, and they both sat in the saddle.

Susan did not drive the wind so hard, this time; the urgency was over, and she did not want to make Roland sick again, even if it had gotten some of the poison out of his system. It was the next morning when they arrived at her father's estate.

She had been gone only a week, but it was longer than she'd ever been gone before, and things had changed, already. There were two little boys running around outside the house, and there was Thunder, slowly digging with a rusted shovel in the place where Father had wanted the new pond. And her father—he was there, taking her up in his arms, as soon as the wind settled.

"I was so worried," he said, "and I couldn't reset that telescope, and I was about to come looking for you, with the boots, but I'm not sure I trust your brother, right now, to be alone with my grandchildren."

Susan nodded, unwrapping Wind-and-Sea and handing her over. "I had the same problem, with Thunder. Do you think—will he—"

"We'll do what we can to set him straight. I've got him on the sort of tasks there's no cheating or magical aid for—hard, honest work will be good for him. And he didn't let this lovely little lady burn; that's what really matters. I see you've got your Roland."

She nodded again, glancing back at him—he was still on the saddle, mostly asleep. It had been a long night, and a longer day before, and he was ill. "I'll set him up in the spare room nearest mine, and come meet my nephews before I go to bed myself—we've been flying through the night."

~

In the morning they had an argument, Roland wanting to be married immediately, and Susan preferring to wait until he could stand on his own feet again without shaking. She had not forgot her disgust at anyone who could hold a wedding for a man so obviously unwell.

In the end they waited a month, which was time enough for Susan's father to make all the grand preparations he'd imagined. He'd been cut out of Thunder's wedding—out of everything to do with Thunder—and had many years' worth of wedding plans saved up.

Her little nephews and her niece were dressed up magnificently, and all their friends from the forest invited, and even Roland's ants, who were set up very carefully in a space where no one would trample them. The bear prince officiated.

It was a lovely wedding, Susan supposed—certainly, her father seemed happy enough. But all she cared for was Roland, his hands in hers, the color finally coming back into his face, looking at her as if she was the only thing in the world worth seeing.

The Shoemaker Prince

His shoes were red. That was the first thing she noticed. There was a man in her tower, and his shoes were red.

There should not have been a man in her tower—her father had been very clear about that. The entire purpose of the tower, in fact, was to prevent men.

"I made them myself," he told her, following her gaze to his feet.

"They're very nice," she said, because what else did one say to a colorful cobbler who had appeared in one's impenetrable fortress?

~

His shoes were red. That was the first thing he noticed. He was sitting in a tree, and his shoes were red.

"Well," he said to himself, as there was no one else about to say it to, "I suppose I had better get down."

He performed a quick inventory at the base of the tree, finding himself utterly unremarkable save the shoes. His clothing was plain, he was quite young, and he carried no luggage. He suspected himself in possession of a name, but could not recall one.

A cardinal landed on one of the lower branches of the tree.

"I suppose," he said to the cardinal, as there was no one else about to say it to, "that I had better find out what's going on here."

There was a clear path ahead; he followed it, and the cardinal followed him, and he discovered quickly that his red shoes were not made for walking.

They came upon the beginnings of a village, and he stopped the first man he saw. "Excuse me, sir. Do you happen to know who I am?"

The man stared for a long moment at the red shoes and at the red bird, which had settled on his shoulder. Then he turned and walked away.

"Well," he said to the cardinal, "it would seem that he doesn't."

The cardinal chirped in response, taking to the air again.

"Onward, then."

In the village, he found himself as much a mystery to everyone else as he was to himself. They sat him in the town square, cardinal atop his head, and gathered about, discussing what to do with him.

"I'm in need of an apprentice," said the candle maker at last, "after that Johnny ran off. We'll keep him in the attic."

And so he was taken with his cardinal to the candle maker's shop, and to the small home above it.

"Red Shoes, we'll call you," said the candle maker's wife, "as we have nothing else to call you. You'll be up with the sun to begin your work."

Red Shoes, as it turned out, was not a good candle maker. Within a week he had been passed on to the grocer, the blacksmith, the lumberjack, the cartographer, the miller, and the tailor, who threw up his arms in despair and declared Red Shoes the most incompetent child he'd ever had the misfortune of meeting.

Finally, they took him to the cobbler, reasoning that at least his shoes may be a novelty for the poor, beleaguered man.

The cobbler was a kind man, but quiet and secluded. He did not need an apprentice, and did not know what to do with a child. He let Red Shoes do as he pleased, and what pleased Red Shoes, more often than not, was running through the woods getting muddy.

But soon winter fell, as winter does, and it was a brutally cold year, driving Red Shoes and his cardinal back to the cobbler's home, where they were constantly underfoot and over head in his shop.

The boy grew, and his feet were pinched and painful in their shoes.

One morning the cobbler called him to the workroom, and on the bench there was sitting a fine piece of red leather.

"We cannot call you Red Shoes if your shoes are not red, and as we have nothing else to call you, red your shoes must remain. But you will learn to make them yourself."

And so the boy became a cobbler. He was not a good cobbler, to start, but as he had nothing better to do through the winter than learn, and nothing to warm his feet until he had, it was not long before he became skilled enough that he was permitted to help making simple shoes for their customers.

The years passed, as years do, and Red Shoes learned his trade, and learned it well, though he would forever rather be outside, with his cardinal in the sky above him. It came one summer that he wished to go adventuring, and the cobbler allowed this. For Red Shoes worked quickly and well, at the times he could be bothered to work at all. The last winter had been a long, restless one, and Red Shoes had worked through all their store of leather, creating shoes of all shape and size. There would be more leather in a sennight, and the cobbler, who was not yet very old, wished to be allowed to do some cobbling of his own; the boy could not hog all the work, he reasoned, if he was off in some other land, fighting dragons or saving princesses, or whatever he imagined he would be doing.

(Likely he would be catching cold from the rain and collecting bruises from sleeping on the ground, and nothing more exciting than that, but the cobbler hadn't the heart to tell him so.)

So off Red Shoes went, into the great wide world, with a new pair of red boots on his feet, and a cardinal resting on his shoulder.

(It was the cardinal that first alerted the village all might not be as it seemed with Red Shoes, for he had been with them ten years that summer, and surely a cardinal should not live so long. But they cared little, what mysteries that elderly bird might hold; Red Shoes was theirs, a charming little ruffian, and a surprisingly good shoemaker besides.)

Red Shoes travelled, over the next several days, for what he imagined was a very great distance indeed, though the cartographer who'd once had the keeping of him, for an hour or so the day after he'd first come to their village, could have told him it was little more than fifty miles. (Red Shoes had been very bad indeed at mapmaking, having invented six new lakes, an island, and several sea monsters to fill them, in the few short minutes he'd been left unattended in possession of a pen.)

Still, fifty miles is not so small a way, when one cannot remember going any farther away than the edges of the forest outside one's own village. And it is true that his feet walked far more than fifty miles, though that was the greatest distance he strayed from home. For Red Shoes was a wanderer born, and strayed often off his intended path, weaving through the land in most peculiar patterns, after whatever happened to catch his eye.

He was stopped, near what he did not know was the fifty-mile mark, by the appearance of a tower suddenly looming before him. It was a very lovely tower indeed, just the sort he might have seen in a picture-book, had there been any picture-books in the part of his childhood he could remember. As there had been no picture-books, the tower took him quite by surprise.

It stood some thirty feet high, which Red Shoes did not know, not having a measuring tape in his pocket, nor knowing the complicated sort of math required to calculate such things from the lengths of the shadows and whatnot. It was made of smooth, lightly colored stones, none of a uniform size, all with lichen growing happily across them.

What interested Red Shoes, though, was the window. He was rather puzzled by the window, as he could see no door—who would be there, to look out the high-up window, if they had no low-down door to enter?

(The cobbler had been a sensible man, and Red Shoes an eccentric child; he had not seen fit to further that eccentricity by feeding it fairy stories.)

Perhaps, Red Shoes thought, the tower was home to large birds, or some sort of winged people, who would have no need for ground-level entry.

(Well, the cobbler did what he could. Red Shoes was always a fantastical child, and if no fantasies were provided, he would create them himself.)

"I suppose," he said to the cardinal, as there was no one else about to say it to, "that we shall have to get up there and see."

(The cobbler had also failed to instill in Red Shoes, despite his best efforts, a respect for private property and aversion to trespassing.)

He climbed the lowest branches of a nearby tree, and sat there for a bit, for he found trees the best place to sit for thinking. As he was not a large bird, nor a person with wings, he was not quite sure how to reach the window.

"This tree," he said the cardinal at last, "is very tall, and it gets quite small and weak-like at the top. I suppose, if I could get up that high, it would just sort of bend down until I could drop into the window."

The cardinal made the particular chirp that meant he felt this a very bad idea. Red Shoes elected to ignore this contribution to the conversation. He climbed the rest of the tree as quickly as he could and, indeed, the higher he climbed, the more it began to bend. And when the angle was just right, he dropped off, and into the open window, bringing him face-to-face with a young woman in a rather bedraggled velvet gown.

~

His shoes were red. That was the first thing she noticed. There was a man in her tower, and his shoes were red.

There should not have been a man in her tower—her father had been very clear about that. The entire purpose of the tower, in fact, was to prevent men.

"I made then myself," he told her, following her gaze to his feet.

"They're very nice," she said, because what else did one say to a colorful cobbler who had appeared in one's impenetrable fortress?

"Thank you," he said, bouncing a little on his toes. A cardinal flew in the window and landed on his shoulder. "I say, do you happen to have wings?"

"I do not," she said, quite baffled. "Do you?"

"No, but my bird does." He sat in the windowsill, making himself quite comfortable in a place he shouldn't have been. "If you haven't any wings, why do you live in a tower that hasn't any doors?"

"My father left me here. So I won't get into any trouble."

He frowned at her. "Well, that's rotten. Life's hardly fun at all, without a little bit of trouble. I get in trouble every day, usually. They've mostly given up yelling at me, now. Only my cardinal was yelling, just now, as much as a cardinal can, because coming up here wasn't the safest, maybe. I'm here now, though, and you're here, and you seem quite nice, so I suppose he'll just have to cope. I like it up here."

"Well, you can't stay. My father shan't like that at all."

"I'm told I'm very likeable."

She shook her head, as firmly as she could manage. "He put me up here to keep me away from all men, so I could never get married and leave him. It doesn't matter how likeable you are, as long as you're a man."

He swung his feet in their bright red shoes, and the cardinal left his shoulder to fly in circles about the room. "I can't help being a man. But I shouldn't like to marry you, anyway—you look rather like a princess, and I would get yelled at something frightful if I brought a princess home to the cobbler. Unless I'd have to go home with you, which would be worse—I'm certain being a prince is ever so much more boring than making shoes."

The young lady, who was, in fact, a princess, was not offended by this; she thought being a prince sounded quite boring, too, and was uninterested in marrying random strangers, besides.

"Perhaps you're in need of rescuing?" he suggested hopefully. "I should like to do some rescuing, as long as I didn't have to marry anyone at the end of it."

The princess considered this. For a father concerned about being left behind, hers certainly seemed to have left her behind— she hadn't seen him in, oh, months and months; it was always servants, now, who came to let food up with the pulley system.

"I shouldn't mind getting out of this tower," she told him. "And then perhaps I could find my missing brothers; surely, if they came home, Father wouldn't be always so anxious and awful anymore."

Red Shoes jumped up from the windowsill, bouncing on his toes again. "I could help find your brothers! I'm very good at finding things. Especially when they're red."

"I don't think my brothers are red," the princess said, though in truth she was a little unsure. They had wandered together into the woods, and never come home, when she and they were all three very small. It could be there was some red to them, like that big, bright scar on her cousin's shoulder, or like her favorite uncle's hair.

"Oh, do say you'll let me help. I've been adventuring for days, and hardly anything exciting has happened at all."

"You can help," the princess allowed, "and we can start by getting out of this dreadful tower." She went to join him at the window, surprised when she looked out to find no waiting rope or ladder. "How do we get out of this dreadful tower?"

Red Shoes wilted. "I suppose I didn't think that far ahead— maybe that's why my bird was squawking so."

"You made a one-way trip into a mysterious tower in the middle of the woods?"

He nodded, looking sheepish.

"Not much of a rescue, then, is it? Well, we've got to find a way down—I'm only given enough food for one, and I'll be in heaps of trouble if anyone finds out you're here."

"Well, how does the food get in?"

"There's a pulley system."

Red Shoes brightened immediately. Pulleys meant ropes, and ropes he could work with. Though, granted, he'd never apprenticed with the rope-maker for even a minute—he'd had ten children of his own, and no intention of taking in a foundling, on top of all that.

"They're ropes strong enough for bringing up food, not people," the princess said.

"Can't know until you've tried," Red Shoes countered, and he tied one end of a rope to her bedpost, and dropped promptly out of the window.

The princess was not altogether surprised when she heard, moments later, a shout and a thud. She leaned out the window.

"Are you all right?" she called down.

"I am," he said, and they stood there for a time, him on the ground, her in the tower, thinking.

"There were several ropes," Red Shoes said at last. "Perhaps if you braided a few of them together, they'd be strong enough to bring you down? Besides, you're probably a bit lighter than me."

The princess made her way down, and they made their way through the forest, in no particular direction, as neither had a clear idea where to go.

"Where were your brothers seen last?" Red Shoes asked, when he could no longer bear to walk in silence.

"In the gardens outside the palace, I suppose. They liked to play in the orchards, but they would sometimes wander too far, until the orchards became the forest."

"I don't suppose they're near the orchards still?"

The princess gave him a withering look. "We've been searching more than ten years, and you think we might have missed them being in our own backyard?"

"Well, you never said it was ten years," Red Shoes countered, and the cardinal chirped in agreement.

"Personally I think they got eaten by a bear the same day we lost them, but Father does rage so if you suggest his precious boys are gone forever." The last time she'd suggested such a thing, she'd also suggested that perhaps she ought to be allowed to get on with living her life, already; her father had responded with a slap at the time, and with the tower a week later.

"Perhaps we could find the bear, and ask him about it?" Red Shoes suggested.

The princess' look became more withering.

"If they're dead, then you'll need a skeleton, or a scrap of clothing. What do princes have—a seal ring or something?"

They stopped for a time, and sat on a large stump to rest, for her shoes were not made for walking. She busied herself with remembering all she could remember of her brothers. This was difficult, as she had spent many years working not to remember, primarily for purposes of spiting her father.

They had been twins, older than her. They had looked exactly alike, and had dressed exactly alike, as well, for one enjoyed causing chaos, and the other enjoyed making his brother happy. The whole kingdom had turned itself upside down in searching, and all anyone had ever found was a single shoe.

"I don't remember any fuss about searching for little princes," Red Shoes says. "That is, well, I wouldn't remember that, as I don't remember much of anything, but I don't remember hearing about any little princes, when I came to my village."

"Not," he added after a moment, as he was an honest enough young man, "that I would have paid much attention, as we've already agreed princes are quite boring."

"Well, it's a quite small kingdom," the princess allowed. "Possibly the matter wasn't quite so pressing for our neighbors."

Red Shoes did not know, as his time with the cartographer had been very brief indeed, that no less than five small kingdoms were spread across the borders of his beloved forest, and that of all of them, only the princess' kept its capital anywhere near the forest at all. Red Shoes did not even know the name of his own kingdom, for its capital lay far, far away from his little village, which hardly bothered at all about anything outside its own small borders, except for when taxes were due.

All the resting in the world would not make a princess' shoes more suitable for walking, and Red Shoes had nothing at hand for cobbling-on-the-go, so they stood and continued on their way. They had been walking for an hour or two, in no particular direction, but quite likely back and forth, or in circles, when the cardinal stirred himself suddenly into a great frenzy, chirping and whistling and flapping his wings wildly.

"Whatever is the matter?" the princess asked, and in response the cardinal swooped low, nearly crashing into her head, then rose up again, flying swiftly away. Red Shoes took off at a run after him, and the princess kept up as best she could, which was not particularly well.

She did not like the thought of Red Shoes getting too far ahead of her, for though they had known each other only a few hours, she had learned enough about him to be wary of the trouble he might find himself in, unsupervised. It was only luck, after all, that had kept him from snapping his neck on his way out of her tower—or on his way into her tower, for that matter.

When she caught up to Red Shoes and the cardinal, they had found an old woman. Unlike Red Shoes, the princess had been raised on picture books and fairy stories, and so recognized the woman as a witch immediately.

"Oh, do be careful, Red Shoes," she said, for it was quite easy to imagine him saying something foolish and getting himself turned into a toad, and how on earth would she manage to find her missing brothers with a toad and a bird to care for, as well as shoes not made for walking?

"You needn't fret," the witch said. "I am here to make things right."

The princess frowned. Who knew what might look right to a witch?

"Do you know where her brothers are?" Red Shoes asked. The cardinal whistled.

The witch raised her eyebrows. "Know where they are? Why, they're right in front of her, you ninny."

"I suppose Red Shoes could be my brother," the princess said. "But I am quite sure there were two of them."

The cardinal, at that moment, swooped down to land on top of Red Shoes' head.

"I am sorry about that," the witch said. "They were such naughty little boys—oh, but little boys are always naughty. It was only supposed to be for a few minutes, and really, being cursed would be an exciting story for a little boy to tell. But I was distracted for just a moment, after I'd transformed the first one, and when I turned back they were both gone. Ten years, and I've finally found you again—I'll have that spell off in a moment."

"My cardinal is my brother?" Red Shoes asked, and the witch nodded.

She waved her hand, and Red Shoes promptly collapsed to the ground, for suddenly there was an entire person sitting on his head.

"I liked being a cardinal," the cardinal said, when both boys had got themselves sorted out and upright again.

"Well," said the witch, "as I've accidently cursed you for ten years, I suppose some compensation is due. You shall be able to change forms, bird and man. How's that?"

He turned instantly back into a cardinal, whistling delightedly.

"Can I be a cardinal, too?" asked Red Shoes.

"No," the princess said firmly.

"Absolutely not," their brother agreed, on the ground and human again. "You're far too scatterbrained to be trusted with a pair of wings; you'd flit off one day and never be seen again."

Red Shoes sighed. He thought he'd make quite a dashing bird.

"If that's all," the witch said," I'll be on my way; I have quite a bit of work to do."

"That is not all," said the princess. "What about Red Shoes? He still hasn't got his memory."

"What's that to do with me? I didn't take the boy's memory."

"Then who did?" asked the princess.

"How should I know? There's plenty of danger about for little boys in the woods. But if you ask me, he's better off without it; being a prince is dreadfully boring."

The witch walked away. The princess looked at Red Shoes. Red Shoes looked at the princess. The cardinal chirped happily in the sky above them.

"I suppose we'd best get you both home to Father, then," the princess said at last, feeling the whole situation rather depressingly anticlimactic.

"But I don't want to be a prince," Red Shoes said.

The cardinal landed again. "We shan't be going back, any of us. I'm the only one Father ever cared about, and I don't care a bit for him. I've seen him hit you, both of you, and we were only little, then; I'm sure he's worse now."

"Then where shall we go?" asked the princess, who did not mind a bit not returning home, but didn't fancy living in the woods for long, either; she had a feeling both of her newly discovered brothers would be quite happy here for far longer than she could put up with.

"Well, we'll go home, of course. I said I'd come back once I'd had my adventure, and I think rescuing a princess and unenchanting a prince is adventure enough. I can make you new shoes!"

"Do they have to be red?"

"I can do any color! I'm good with dyes."

"And the cobbler won't mind, having a princess underfoot?"

"Well, he got used to having the two of us underfoot—or overhead, I suppose. Anyway, he'll manage. After all, you're very likeable. I quite liked you already, even before you were my little sister."

"You can learn a trade as well, if you're worried about being a burden," suggested the cardinal, who had always been the more practical, down-to-earth twin, despite being a bird. "The grocer still doesn't have an apprentice."

"I quite like groceries," said the princess.

And so it was settled, and the three of them made their way home, the shoemaker prince, the grocer princess, and a cardinal flying happily above their heads.

The Man Who Forgot How to Love

His beloved had fallen ill, a wasting sickness for which no physician could find a cure.

He had left behind everything he had ever known to stand by her side, had given up the crown that should have been his to live in a strange land surrounded by strangers, his betrothed one of only three people in the country who spoke his language. He had promised her everything he had, everything he was, and she would not live past the end of the year.

He could not lose her. He would not. The world was a large, mysterious place; if there was no cure in this land, there may be one in some other. If doctors and science could not save her, perhaps witches and magic could. And so he packed a small bag, kissed her fevered brow, and set out across the sea to save her.

It took him many weeks to travel far enough for a cure—many frantic weeks, when every hour counted, when she might be dead at home already. He had reached a frenzied state of panic by the time he reached a witch in a far distant land who claimed to have what he needed.

She was a withered old woman, with an aching sadness hung about her.

"The price is very high," the witch said.

"I will pay anything."

"Do not be hasty, little prince," she said softly. "I would spare you both from this, if I could."

He was not a prince, not anymore; he had given that up, to be with her, and would give up anything else just as willingly. "What will it cost?" he asked.

"The price of saving her is the love you bear her."

A very high price, then. He had—he had not expected that. But better, surely, for him to lose her—for her to lose him—than for her to lose her life.

He nodded. The witch sighed, then waved her hand.

"It is done," she said.

He was consumed, for a moment, by a deep, burning emptiness, which faded into a dull ache.

"Thank you," he said, because he was a polite young man, even when the most precious thing he had was unceremoniously stripped away. He did not wish to linger in the place where it happened. "I must be returning to her, then."

The witch looked surprised. "You're going back?"

"Of course," he said. "I made a promise. And how else will I know you've held up your end of the bargain?"

The witch smiled at him, a bright, genuine thing that reminded him of his grandmother. "You will be all right, I think," she said. "Wait here; I'll get you some food for your journey home."

He made his way back to his—not his beloved, anymore. His betrothed, then. She was still betrothed, if not beloved. He made his way back to her, worrying at the empty space in his heart, not quite sure how he felt, anymore. He tried to think of her, to pull up all the warmest, happiest feelings, but his thoughts would skitter quickly away. It was—he had to see her, had to hold her hands in his. He felt—but surely love was too great a thing to be simply stripped away. He would see her, and the feelings would come flooding back, and all would be right again.

He travelled less quickly, on the return journey; the sense of urgency had faded, and all his best efforts could not call it back. But when he finally made his way there, his betrothed was standing on her own feet, as she had not in so long, with her hair pulled back and dressed in a simple everyday gown.

He waited for the great welling up of feelings he always felt when he saw her, but there was nothing. Only a yawning sort of emptiness. He ignored it, and went to embrace her, and told her that it would be better, now, that he had found a cure. He had made a promise, and he would not let it be broken by a bit of magic. It wasn't as if he loved anyone else, in her place.

So he threw himself into her recovery, holding her arm as they walked slowly through the gardens, seeing to it that she ate enough each meal, that she slept enough each night. They did not speak of their wedding, but they had not, really, since she first fell ill—let her recover fully, he thought, and then they could face that problem.

No. It was not a problem at all. He had made a promise. He would keep his promise. There was no one else for him to marry, and it wasn't as if he felt any sort of animosity toward her. He felt— he did not know how to categorize his feelings. He remembered how love had felt, and it had not felt like this. But as to what he felt instead—he had not quite worked that out, yet. It was not exactly nothing, but it was not exactly something, either.

Alas, his betrothed was not an unobservant woman.

"You don't love me anymore," she said quietly one day, as they sat on a bench in the garden, taking in the sun. "Do you?"

"Of course I do," he said, and it was the first lie he had ever told her.

"Is it—is it because I'm different?"

"No," he said.

It was true that she had changed. She seemed to have aged ten years in the last two. There was a new asymmetry to her face, her left eye never opening quite as wide, the left side of her mouth always slightly turned down. She was still too pale and too thin, and moved in a fumbling, fragile way. The hearing in her left ear was gone, and at times she became confused, or got lost a bit in her head. The illness had been very bad, and the fever had burned through her nerves and into her brain.

He still found her beautiful, though it had never been her beauty that he had loved.

"I don't care about any of that," he said, which was true.

"I will love you forever," he said next, which was not true at all. But he would have; oh, he would have, if he had not had to save her.

"I don't believe you," she said quietly, and there was a bottomless sadness in her eyes, which reminded him strangely of the witch.

"I will prove it," he promised, with no idea how he would do so. He wanted—he wanted so badly to love her still. But magic was a funny thing, and the spot she'd held in his heart was empty.

Empty things, he told himself, could be refilled. And why could he not fill it back up with her?

They took walks in the garden, short, then longer, then longer still, as her strength returned. He braided her hair each night before she went to bed, first because her hands shook too much to do it herself, and then because it had become a habit, a ritual between them. He learned not to approach her from the left, as it tended to startle her badly.

Spring came, and she seemed to blossom back into herself—still changed, still weaker than she had been, but healing and happy to be alive.

"You needn't still marry me, you know," she said one evening, and his hands stilled in her hair. "It was a promise made long ago, and I imagine we were both different people, then."

He resumed his braiding. "I want to marry you."

"But do you love me?"

There was a pause, as he carefully twisted her hair. And the words burst out of him, suddenly, taking him by surprise. "Yes. Yes, I love you."

"Darling…"

"Love may be a feeling, but it is also a choice. And I choose you. To be yours. Forever, and longer still."

"Are you sure?" she asked.

"Yes," he said. "Yes. The witch took something out of me, in exchange for saving you. I do not know what it was. She said it was love. Maybe it was, of a sort. But I think—I think it was not the sort of love that lasts, through long, slow years and painful things. Because I came back. Because I was afraid to tell you what had happened, what it had cost me—and why should I care about hurting you, about losing you, if I did not love you still? We may both be different people, now. But I want to stand beside you, and see all the different people you will ever be. And I think all the different people I will ever be shall still love you—maybe not in the same way. Maybe there are different kinds of love for different versions of ourselves. Maybe the kind of love the witch took out of me will never come back. But I still love you. She took away all the grand, dramatic things. But I still love you in all the quiet, simple ways that are good for growing old with, and I want to stay with you."

She turned to face him, dislodging his hands from her hair, and she smiled at him, a slowly unfolding thing that felt like sunrises and blooming roses and the smell of the sea in the air. "We'll get married, then," she said.

And they did.

Windows

We used to be rich. Well, relatively. I used to have my own laptop and cell phone and college tuition money. Then Mom died. Then Dad lost his job. Then Dad lost all my tuition money, and just about everything else. Mom always warned him not to mess with the stock market.

For a while everything hurt too much to matter. Then I tried being angry. Then understanding—it was just one bad choice. It could have happened to anyone. He's half mad with grief. He'll feel bad about it later. But that just made me more angry, until I was tired of being angry, and now I'm just tired. So this'll be good. Something new. Forget the money, because that will never make this better, but it'll be nice to get away from here.

We leave home at dawn the day after I graduate. I have one backpack to bring, and no friends to say goodbye to. Dad's driving me in a borrowed car, and we don't talk.

We lost everything.

This job he's taking me to—nannying or housekeeping or tutoring or something—I don't know how he found it, and I don't think he knows what it even is—I'll be living there. For a year. A year and a day, which is beyond weird, but I signed a contract and everything, and the pay is good. Dad'll be fine while I'm gone. And Pam and Mary, who were safely at college, their tuition safely paid, when the world collapsed.

The sky is still periwinkle, just starting to turn pink around the edges, and I'm wearing my red sundress and gladiator sandals, which are the only nice clothes to survive the ordeal. Gotta look presentable for the boss.

If he wants me to have clean hair he'd better provide the shampoo—no room in the backpack or the budget.

I count the minutes—thirty eight—that we drive without seeing any houses. Dad never said it would be way out in the country. But then he never really said anything.

I hope this guy's not a perv. Twenty minutes of nothing, twenty minutes of freaking driveway—I'm completely cut off from everything.

Dad doesn't even walk me to the door. I remind myself, again, of the mad with grief thing, and try to say "goodbye," and "I love you," but I'm really not in the mood, so I just leave, and pretend not to notice when he drives away before I even reach the house.

It's a huge, sprawling thing, vaguely colonial, with chipped paint and overgrown grass, half alive and not quite ominous. There's a sign on the door inviting me in, and I obey.

Everything is filthy, and not a single one of the nine light bulbs above me flicks on. There are probably rats in a house like this. Or at least mice. Possibly bats, definitely spiders. People seem unlikely.

It takes me half an hour to find the kitchen, which is spotless and well-lit and familiar, with rows of dark hickory cabinets and a small square table at the center of the room. Signs of life. Finally. For a moment I think it's a miracle, and then I see him.

He's sitting at the far end, hands folded in his lap, dark hair falling over his eyes, clothes thirty years out of style, squinting slightly.

His trunk hangs down onto the table.

You did not misread that sentence.

People talk about Elephant Man. Well, that was all a pretty rough situation, I guess. But he didn't actually look anything like an elephant. There's unfortunate physical deformities, and then there's going and stealing body parts from other species.

He's about my age, very pale, with a narrow face mostly dominated by the trunk.

"Are you Regina?"

His voice is soft, and he picks up the trunk as he speaks, playing with it like I might play with my hair, and I realize he's afraid of me.

Well, the feeling is mutual.

I cross my arms and try to sound tough while backing away. "Yeah. Reggie. What do you want with me?"

He stands and comes forward, much too close, and I hit the wall and stop backing up. "He didn't tell you," he says.

The trunk. He didn't tell me about the trunk—did he know about the trunk? You can't just not mention trunks. People do not have trunks. People do not have trunks.

He has a trunk.

He reaches out with it, and I say "Don't touch me," just too late to stop it brushing against my shoulder. He flinches away, and starts running his hands over it, and I start straightening my dress, wishing for pockets to cram my hands into, because I'm tempted to do the same thing with my braid.

It was too leathery to be human, but somehow more human than elephant still, and when he lifted it up I saw he had tiny tusks. Nothing like crooked human teeth. I know tusks when I see them. These are tusks.

I could leave still. I could—it's an hour away. Dad dropped me off. He dropped me off—he knew—and he didn't even wait to see if I got to the door. He just—he—I'm halfway down the hall, anyway, thinking maybe I can walk or something, before it really sinks in that I'm alone here. I hunch over. Deep breaths, Reggie. Deep breaths. I stand up, push my shoulders back. He's here, he followed me—of course he followed me—and I'm fine. Everything is fine. Trunk. No big deal.

"I didn't know you didn't know," he whispers. "You can go home if you like."

"Not unless you can drive me."

"I don't go outside."

Somehow that doesn't surprise me. "Guess I'm stuck, then. A year and a day, right? So how does this thing work?"

And this is what I get for not reading the contract. There must have been an elephant clause, or something. At least I'm not so worried about the perv factor anymore. Give me some time to adjust to the whole facial thing, but he seems too shy to be making any kind of inappropriate moves.

"You can have whatever room you like. Things are kind of a mess. But anything you want. It doesn't matter."

"But what am I supposed to do?" He stares at me like I'm the weird one here, and I start speaking very slowly. "You hired me. So what's my job? What do you want me to do?"

It's gotta be housekeeping.

"You were just going to be here."

He sounds so pathetic when he says it. But I don't want to just be here. That's weird. You can't pay a person for living with you. Not unless you can't take care of yourself, or you're doing something sketchy. Trunk possession doesn't seem debilitating, and I will be doing nothing sketchy.

"Uh huh. That's great. You got a lawn mower? How about a broom? Mop? Spare light bulbs?"

He shrugs. "Somewhere around. Probably. Dad knows where everything is."

Dad. So we're not alone. This guy's just the welcoming committee. "And where is Dad?"

"Gone."

"Well, when will he be back?"

"I don't know."

"Okay." Really helpful, this guy. "Guess I'll just go pick a room then. Where are you?"

The trunk lifts, and I see him frown around the tusks. "Right here?"

"No. Where do you sleep? And what's your name, while we're at it?"

"In Dad's room. It's over there." He points vaguely to the left with his trunk. "I'm Elton."

Seriously? Like the kid wasn't doomed enough with the trunk and the tusks? Elton. That's probably as bad as Regina.

Something to bond over, though. Maybe. I don't quite have the guts to point it out—he seems like the kind of guy who might not even realize Elton is a crappy name. I mean, he's dressed like it's nineteen ninety three, so his standards can't be high.

And what kind of a freak shares a room with his dad?

Wait. Does the dad have a trunk, too? At least now I know why I'm getting paid so much.

I pick a room on the second story, with a lock on the door, and start clearing out the junk. Everything goes across the hall—a large collection of silk flowers, a stuffed monkey with his tail coming unstitched. Sixteen VHS tapes, and none of them movies worth seeing.

The light is burned out, and the sheets are probably dirty. It wouldn't hurt to vacuum and clean the windows.

I'm officially declaring myself housekeeper. The pay is ridiculous, even for trunks; I can't just sit here keeping him company for twelve months. Anyway, I don't do company. Not since Mom died, and not with weird guys who don't know their own species or when their dads will be home.

It takes three hours and eighteen rooms to find a linen closet. Lunch gets skipped. No sign of Elton. Another forty five minutes to find a washing machine, which doesn't look like it's been used lately. At least there's still detergent. I change my sheets and strip all the beds I've seen so far. Next step: find and clean bathrooms. After that: find Elton.

When it gets to be dinner time I head back to the kitchen, which is harder to find than it should be. Elton wanders in just as I'm discovering that the contents of his fridge have all gone bad. Like maybe he bought them in the same year he bought that shirt he's wearing. That bad.

I'm not thinking about the trunk. Not thinking about it. Just pretend it isn't there.

"When's the last time you went shopping?"

"Never. Dad does the shopping."

"Right. And when did Dad leave, exactly?" This is getting weird. It's late. He should have been here when I got here.

"Nine months ago," Elton says.

Well. That sort of changes things.

Absent parents are always a touchy subject, and Elton's trunk is flicking in a way I don't like—maybe I'll wait to get to know him before I ask where he went. Did he die? Did he just walk out? But more importantly: "What have you been eating, then? It can't be this stuff. You're clearly not dead from food poisoning."

He opens a cupboard to reveal cans. Lots and lots of cans.

"Great. That's nice. We're going to the grocery store tomorrow."

"Okay."

"Do you have dirty laundry? Are your sheets clean? Do you know where the vacuum is? Do you have any shampoo?"

"Yes and no and no and no."

"Okay. Bring the dirty stuff to the washing machine. I'll get you new sheets. And canned food. Honestly. How are you even still alive?"

He shrugs.

The next day he presents me with a ludicrous amount of cash, and I find a garage with a rundown car inside. Thank God it has gas.

It takes me an hour to find civilization and a store, and by then I'm halfway home, and consider just finishing it—he paid in advance, the grocery money could get me a laptop, and we could keep the crappy car. Elton's not following me if I leave. But there are only so many cans left. He'd starve, eventually. And at least there's something to do here, besides count money we don't have and get stared at by people who used to actually talk to me.

Speaking of staring. Cashiers give me weird looks when I count out Elton's stupid wad of cash. But I guess he'd get weirder ones.

I behave myself. Shampoo, two T-shirts, and a pair of tennis shoes. Nothing else just for me.

~

After a couple weeks he's transitioned from the nineties to the seventies. I suspect him of working backwards through his father's wardrobe. It probably got to be a habit, after all those months alone, when apparently he can't run a washing machine. I clean everything remotely contemporary, stack it outside his door, and hope for results.

The ground level has now been vacuumed, and I've lost count of all the rooms. I'm wondering if it's only a coincidence that Elton's ears are on the large side.

He's both dangerously trusting and bizarrely paranoid. I know where he keeps his money—hundreds of thousands of dollars in cash—and I'm encouraged to take whatever I like for shopping, and buy whatever I want. But he balks at cleaning the windows. Filth is safer.

"Someone could see inside," he says, arms folded and trunk flicking.

"Who? There's nothing for miles."

"What if someone drove past?"

"Yeah. Good point. You know that forty minute drive to civilization?" He nods. "Half of that is your driveway, Elton."

I go to get the ladder I've seen in the garage, and he follows me to the door, then stops at the threshold, muttering in gibberish. Or some language I don't know, at least. It sounds like gibberish.

He does that. It's irritating. "Elton?"

"Clean the windows. Whatever. I can't—clean them yourself. I'll wait here."

"When's the last time you were outside, Elton?"

"The day Dad left."

"Oh."

"It was the first time I ever went outside."

I didn't want to know that. I didn't need to know that. I am not here to provide abandonment counseling for elephant boy—I just want to wash the freaking windows.

Well, I don't, really. I hate heights. But I also hate not being able to see past a year's worth of dirt. So.

"There's nothing out there. Just come hold the bottom of the ladder for me."

He won't do it. I go alone, praying I won't lose my balance and die, and he avoids rooms with windows for the rest of the day.

Some mornings I'll find him sitting at a window, now that they're clean, staring longingly out. "You could go outside, you know."

He looks up. "Dad would kill me."

"Your dad's not here, Elton." He's moved back up to the eighties outfits. I'm trying very hard to see that as a good thing—at least we're moving in the right direction. He starts tugging at his trunk, the way he does when he's anxious.

"He would kill me," he repeats.

"Elton…"

He stands and walks towards the fridge—we're in the kitchen. We're always in the kitchen. It's his favorite room; I guess I should have known that when I walked in and it wasn't under an inch of dust.

"I should learn to cook. Shouldn't I? I mean, you'll only be here another ten months." He opens the cookbook I bought last week, and holds it maybe an inch from his face, squinting.

"How are you going to get food to cook?"

"Right. Well, I always liked canned corn." He slides down to sit on the floor, trunk drooping.

I leave him there—the entire top floor is still unvacuumed, and I have more important things to do than feel sorry for Elton.

~

A week later I walk in on him doing—I don't know what he's doing. The monkey I found on the first day has migrated into his room, and it's sitting on the bed. There are pictures of him and a guy who must be his dad on the wall—no trunk, if you were wondering—and the sheets on his bed are tangled, and there's a pile of dirty clothes in the corner. It's such a nice, human little room, and the way he's moving his trunk right now, and the sounds coming out of it—he's never seemed less human. It's stretched out and trumpeting and elephantine and I remember for the first time in weeks that I used to be afraid of him.

When he sees me in the door he stops, and we just stare at each other for a while. He picks up the monkey with his trunk, and flings it across the room, then he lowers his trunk, very slowly, still staring at me. The whites of his eyes are pink. He's been crying. The trumpet sound is crying.

Crap.

"What are you?"

"I don't know."

I meant to ask him what was wrong. Honestly I did.

"You need to mow the lawn." It was why I'd come looking for him in the first place, and as good a way as any to change the subject.

"I don't know how."

"You have a riding mower. I'm not heavy enough to keep it running."

"I can't go outside."

"You don't have any neighbors. No one will see anything. Mow the lawn, Elton."

"I can't."

I pick up the monkey and hand it to him. "We should sew the tail back on. What's that picture from?"

He moves forward and squints at the one I'm pointing to. "My birthday. I was eight. Dad burned the cake."

Half an hour later we go to the garage, and I help him get the mower running.

~

He doesn't have a phone, or a computer, or anything. It doesn't take long to convince him that we both need cells, but if he can live without the internet I guess I can too.

Sometimes I catch him trying to dial the phone with his trunk, which is ridiculous, and he shoves it into his pocket—the phone, not the trunk—if he notices me. I wonder who he's trying to call, when I'm the only person he interacts with, and I'm standing in the next room.

His dad left over a year ago, and all the laundry in the house is clean. He's still wearing bellbottom jeans a size too big.

I get it. Some days I almost call my dad. He doesn't make any contact himself, but then how would he, when I came here with no phone or laptop?

"You never get any mail."

Elton shrugs. "We have a box at the post office."

"A box that hasn't been checked in a year?" He nods. "Really, Elton? Get me the key. I'll do it tomorrow."

He presents me with a huge key ring, and it takes seven tries to find the one I need, and people are giving me weird looks again. And of course, there's nothing from Dad. From either of our dads. Just a bunch of overdue bills. Elton reads them all very carefully, squinting, then counts out the money I'll need to pay them.

~

You wouldn't expect the bills to be so high, when she was dead before they even got her to the hospital. Stupid icy roads. But funeral expenses and everything, I guess. Anyway, it wasn't devastating. Not financially. It was just—that was when Dad got reckless. I like that Elton doesn't ask me about any of it—weird, I guess, to love how completely uninterested someone is in your life. He still isn't telling what happened with his dad, and I still don't have the guts to ask.

I have found out he was homeschooled (duh), eighteen years old, and the language he mumbles in sometimes is ancient Greek. Weirdo. It's crazy the things he knows. And loves. Like math and botany. But no one ever taught him common sense. In the nine months that he was alone, he lived exclusively in the kitchen and his father's bedroom, and didn't bother to keep the bedroom clean. Or to do anything, really. Good thing they had so much food in cans.

He cheats at board games. He's learning to cook. I can usually get him to go outside at least once a week.

Sometimes when I have bad hair days, he'll promise, from across the room, that I look very nice. It would be sweet, except that I know he can't see me from there. He refuses to go to an eye doctor.

~

The day after the first snow we trudge outside, him in his dad's ancient snow gear, me in something he paid for. One of these days I'm going to find out where they got all that money.

It takes him five minutes to discover he can throw snowballs with his trunk. Cheater. I retaliate, and wait for the trunk to go numb. I told him to wrap it in a scarf or something.

He manages to hit me nearly every time, and I'm starting to suspect him of faking six months of blindness.

"You're wearing bright red," he tells me.

"I could take you to get glasses tomorrow."

He throws another snowball.

~

"You should take a break, Reggie."

I'm lying on the floor, eyes closed, and when I open them to see him hanging over me, I use the trunk to pull myself to my feet.

"A break?"

"Go visit your family or something. For Christmas. You're half done, right? And you haven't had a single day off."

"I don't do anything to take a break from."

"You put up with me. And you cleaned the entire house."

I shrug. "I'm good."

He frowns, but lets it go. I don't mind being here, really. I don't—half elephant roommate. It's like a freaking fairy tale. I mean, really bizarre and noticeably lacking in pretty dresses and charming princes, but I'll take it over real life. And I'm not entirely sure Elton, with his new interest in cooking, wouldn't burn down the house if I left him alone for a weekend.

Nine months this boy lived alone. Nine months.

And in another six I'm leaving him alone again. Forever.

Well, it's not as if I can just stay here.

~

59

"I could teach you to drive," I offer when the snow is melting and I can count the months left on one hand.

"Where would I go?"

"Wherever you wanted to."

"I can't go out in public."

"Just for something to do, Elton. Aren't you bored? All your movies suck, we don't have cable, and we've played every game you own a dozen times."

"You could read."

"Yeah. Or you could drive."

He learns fast, and frets about getting caught without a license, never mind that we never even manage to leave his enormous driveway. The trunk alternates between helping and getting in the way, and I fail to convince him to come into town.

"We could get you glasses, and you could actually see the road."

"I'm fine."

"You've run over a squirrel and a rabbit this morning, Elton."

"I'm fine," he says again.

"The rabbit and the squirrel aren't." He doesn't answer. "We could get you a permit. A license. You could buy your own groceries when I'm gone."

That was a mistake—we don't talk about when I'm gone. Not anymore. Everything gets very quiet, and he parks the car in the garage.

"You're right. It really isn't safe for me to drive, is it?"

"Elton, don't."

"Don't what? Slaughter rodents? Yeah, I'll just kill them all."

"Don't storm off and pretend you can keep living like this."

"I can't. That's the point. You're leaving in two months now, Reggie."

"So leave with me. Do something. Live."

"Dad—"

"Would kill you. I know. Your dad's not coming back, Elton." We're in the garage now, outside the car. He stares at me for a minute, trunk hanging eerily still, then goes inside. The door slams.

It's the first time I've ever seen his bedroom door closed. I knock—no answer—and turn the knob. Turns out he has a lock, too.

"Elton, come on." I could apologize. Maybe I should. But instead I say, "It's been a year and a half. Quit moping."

He doesn't answer. He doesn't come out for dinner. I give up and go to bed, and in the morning he doesn't come out for breakfast, either. It's nearly noon when he emerges, in normal jeans and a T shirt, everything the right size.

"What's for lunch?"

I hand him a soup can, and he squints and brings it close to read. "I thought you banned the cans."

"Well, I figured if you're going back to this when I—might as well start readjusting now, right?"

He sets the can down. "It's not like I look a little funny, Reg. You know the Minotaur?" I do, unfortunately. He's told me all the Greek myths, and if I stay here much longer I'm sure he'll start on the language, too. "Sometimes I wonder. How that all happened, with Pasiphae and everything. I never met my mom."

"That's not even remotely—I mean, even if offspring was a genetic possibility, there's no way you could ever—the size difference."

"I know that. I just meant—I can't just walk down the street. I'll end up in a zoo."

"Well, you can't just stay here alone your whole life, either."

I don't know how long I've known I would stay here with him. It seems inevitable. I have to—I can't just abandon him the way I guess his dad must have. Like I guess my dad did to me. But I don't exactly love the idea of giving up my entire life because I have a lonely friend.

"You could get plastic surgery."

"Sure. Except do you honestly think that wasn't the first thing they tried nineteen years ago?"

He didn't tell me when he turned nineteen. But then, I didn't tell him when I did, either. "Medicine's advanced a lot since then."

"I can't, Reggie. I can't."

"Okay. So we'll figure something else out. We will. I promise. Maybe you could grow a huge beard."

"Perfect. You're a genius." He opens the fridge. "Maybe stir fry."

~

The vintage clothes don't resurface. We don't mention his father again, or the fact that I'm leaving. Sometimes I try to say things about computers, and food delivery services, but he just twists his trunk and looks away. We don't go driving again.

It's a huge house, and I still get lost in it after a year. Finding him is harder and harder lately—he's really branched out since those early days when he lived out of two rooms. If you can call that living. There's a week and a day left on my contract when I find him, after two hours of searching, in a third story bedroom playing chess with himself. Hands black, trunk white.

"Who's winning?"

He doesn't look up. "Take me to the eye doctor, Reggie."

"What?"

"You're the only friend I've ever had, you're leaving in a week, and I've never really seen you. Take me to the eye doctor."

I rush him to the car before he has time to change his mind. The departure date, with its sense of urgency, is largely hypothetical— I'm depending on Dad, who I haven't spoken with in twelve months, to come and get me, and if he hasn't checked up in all this time then I might very well be stuck here forever. But I'll take any opportunity Elton gives me. The boy needs glasses.

It takes fifteen minutes to get us farther from the house than Elton's ever been. It takes twenty five before he's hunched over, head between his knees, just in case we drive past anyone else.

"There's no one here. It'll be fifteen minutes before we see a house." His trunk comes up towards my knee, which is probably the only answer I'm going to get. "You know the doctor will have to see you when we get there."

"We'll find a blind one."

"A blind eye doctor? Good luck with that."

It occurs to me as we reenter civilization that I should probably have called to make an appointment. It also occurs to me that I should probably lock Elton's door—he looks about ready to bolt and head home, which is stupid because he'll only be seen by more people if he leaves the car.

I think I know where to find an ophthalmologist in this town, but it's sort of touch and go. I may have driven past the place a couple times. Maybe. Probably. Groceries and clothes and cell phones were obvious, and I never felt the need to investigate further.

He's mumbling something in Greek. That's never a good sign. "Elton?"

"Let's go back."

"We're not even there yet."

"Good. It was a stupid idea. Let's go home."

Just as he says that I see the sign. Eye doctor. I pull into the parking lot. "Sit up. It's fine; no one's here." I grab his trunk the way I would his hands if they were more accessible, and he rises slowly, glancing out the window every few seconds. "It's fine, Elton."

"I've never actually seen a real parking lot before."

"Nice, isn't it?"

"What will you do? Next week, I mean. Will you go to school?"

"I never applied."

"Next semester, then. Or you could get a real job, or travel a lot. You could do anything. What do you want to do?"

We don't talk about when I leave. But eight days. I guess we have to. "I want to get you glasses."

"That's not a practical life goal, Reggie."

"I'm not leaving until you can see."

"If you're still trying to convince me to go to the doctor today, then you're doing an exceptionally terrible job of it."

"What happened to your dad, Elton?"

"He's gone."

"I know that. Where'd he go?"

"He's not coming back."

I knew that already, too, but maybe he didn't. "I'm sorry."

"Who would? I'm—I don't even know what I am. It doesn't matter."

"I would. I will. I have to—you're my best friend, and you've never really seen me." I don't have to give up my whole life. But I can definitely come back. To visit. Holidays. Weekends. Mondays and Tuesdays and Wednesdays. Maybe Thursdays.

"Right." He takes a deep breath. "I guess we should go in."

"I guess so."

He straightens out his trunk, then just sits there, staring out the window, one hand on the door handle. A car drives past, then another one. He doesn't react.

I don't know if we'll make it inside today. I don't even know if we'll make it out to the parking lot. I don't say anything—I can wait.

The Princess Who Refused to Marry a Merman

Once there was a lovely princess who had been imprisoned in an island palace. The prince she loved would visit her when he could, but he could not visit often, nor could he save her. For he had been turned into a bluebird, and it was a long flight for little wings.

The princess had one steady companion over the long months of her confinement; this was a mermaid who dwelt in the sea below the palace. They had become very dear friends, but the mermaid wished to be dearer still—she wanted the princess to be not just a friend, but a sister.

It happened that the mermaid had a brother, and she wished him to marry the princess. She did not care that the princess had already given her heart to another, for mermaids are selfish, soulless things.

Now, while all mermaids are beautiful creatures, all mermen are hideously ugly, and her brother was no exception. The princess consented to meet the merman, only to be polite, but he was so ugly that she could scarcely bear to look at him.

She explained to the mermaid, as politely as she could, that she could not possibly marry her brother, never mentioning his ugliness, but only her love for the bluebird prince.

The mermaid was enraged. She summoned all of her friends from the depths of the sea, and they set about flooding the palace, for she was determined to drown the princess.

The princess took herself to the highest tower of the palace, searching for escape, as the lower levels filled with water. Looking out the window, she saw the merman whom she had so recently rejected, beckoning her frantically.

She did not wish to marry him. But if he was offering her an escape—surely, they could agree to some payment other than her hand, once she was safely away from here.

The water rose and rose, until it came flowing through her window, which had that morning been high among the clouds. The merman swam in and took her hand, pulling her quickly out of the palace and to the new, much-risen surface of the sea.

He did not speak. He had not spoken when his sister introduced them, either; she thought he must not know their language. She certainly did not know his.

She did not know where he was taking her, nor what he intended to do with her, but as long as she was not yet drowned, there was hope for escape.

~

The merman was annoyed. His sister wished him to marry this strange, land-bound person; his sister often had peculiar ideas of this sort. He did not care to marry the strange, land-bound person, and did not think she cared to marry him, either. Drowning the poor girl was certainly uncalled-for.

His sister knew he had a softer heart than many of their species. Likely she had planned this knowing he would feel obligated to rescue her, thus forcing them to spend time together. But they could not communicate, and the girl appeared—quite understandably— afraid.

There was an island not far from here. Hopefully he could leave her there with creatures of her own sort.

~

The merman swam for many hours, pulling the princess steadily along. She knew nothing of his intentions, only that every mile they swam took her farther away from her darling bluebird prince, who would not know how to find her again.

At last they reached land, and the princess scrambled quickly to shore as soon as she felt sand beneath her feet.

The merman nodded, waved, and disappeared into the sea.

Thus abandoned by her unwanted suitor, the princess wrung the water from her skirts and her hair, and walked in the direction of a few small buildings just visible in the distance.

Her shoes had been lost in the sea, and the salt and the wet had left her gown in poor condition. She was very tired, for they had travelled what seemed a great distance, and she had always been a poor swimmer. But her greatest concern was for her prince, who, when next he made the long and difficult journey to see her, would find only a flooded palace, and would surely think her dead.

Night had fallen by the time she reached civilization, where she found a group of people who spoke her language no better than the merman had. One was kind enough to offer, by pantomime, a space for her to sleep that night, as well as a new dress and a pair of shoes.

Grateful, the princess departed early the following morning, not wishing to further impose. She must find her bluebird, before he failed to find her. Surely, now that she had been freed, in however unlikely a manner, from her prison, she could learn how to free him from the spell he was under.

She wandered far, for many days. Alas, the land where the merman had left her was an island, and when she realized this, she made plans to earn herself passage on a ship to the continent.

The sailors were wary, as sailors often are, of having a woman on board. But she excelled, after many years imprisoned in a palace alone, at such tasks as cooking and cleaning and mending, and when she fixed a torn sail and made a fine stew in the same hour, they consented to take her on board, for all of these sailors hated mending, and were very poor cooks indeed.

They sailed for nearly a week before disaster struck. The mermaid had not forgotten her anger at the princess, and when she sensed that the girl was again on the sea, she went to confront her, bringing along a terrible storm which she had tamed and kept as a pet.

She came upon the princess late at night, when most of the crew was asleep. The princess was often up at this hour; she liked to stare out at the stars when all was still and quiet, wondering where in the endless expanse of sky her bluebird might be.

The mermaid entreated the princess, again, to marry her brother, and the princess again refused. The mermaid responded by setting her pet storm upon the ship, which quickly woke the sleeping sailors.

The storm raged on for many minutes, and all aboard feared for their lives. The sailors saw the mermaid watching from the sea, and knew she had set the storm, though they did not know why.

As they watched, a hideously ugly merman rose from the waters, and began arguing fiercely with the mermaid in his own language. Though she was clearly quite displeased, the mermaid at last called off the storm and slid beneath the waves. The merman waved to the princess before following her, and the princess waved cheerily back.

For some minutes the sailors stood about the deck, stunned at the now-stilled ocean. They discussed the mermaid and the storm, while the princess tried to stay quietly out of the way, knowing that it was all her fault. But none of the sailors had witnessed her argument with the mermaid, and at length they concluded that she had, by her great beauty and kindness, charmed the ugly merman who called off the storm, and that they therefore all owed her their lives.

The princess was afraid to tell the truth, and so accepted their gratitude. And when their captain died of a sudden fever a few days later, they all elected to make her their new leader, for surely a captain who could protect them from scurvy and mermaids both was the best sort of captain to have.

She did not forget her bluebird prince. But captaining a ship, it turned out, took quite a lot of work, and so she was forced, for a time, to set her search aside. She led her sailors on many grand journeys, doing her best to be a good captain, but always she worried for her prince, who must by now believe her dead.

When she had been a captain for nearly two years, they reached for the first time a land that looked somewhat familiar to her. When she went to the market for fresh fruit—for she was very determined that none of her sailors should have scurvy—she recognized, on the coins the fruit-seller handled, the face of her bluebird's older brother.

All plans for fruit abandoned, she made her way quickly to the palace to search for news of her beloved. But alas, she had no way to prove her identity, and the king refused to see her. She returned to her ship, and told her sailors, for the first time, the truth of her life before meeting them. They determined at once to help her find her lost prince, and that night, when the king went for a walk in his gardens before bed—which the princess knew, being engaged to his brother, had been a daily habit of his from childhood—the sailors grabbed him, and smuggled him quickly down to the docks.

Brought face to face with the princess, the king recognized her as his brother's beloved, and quite forgot to be angry at the kidnapping. He told the princess that his brother, finding her home destroyed and no evidence that she still lived, had given up all hope of his spell ever being broken. For what did it matter, whether he was a man or a bird, if he did not have her?

The king had begged the prince not to give up, but he could not be reasoned with, and had sold himself to a zoo, to live out the rest of his days as a simple bird. And, not wanting his brother to spoil his plans, he had chosen a zoo well outside the furthest reaches of his kingdom, the name of which the king did not know.

The sailors returned the king to his palace, and the princess decided, with their support, that they would abandon their stock of exotic foods and fine fabrics and all the things a merchant ship usually carried, and deal from now on in the transport and sale of animals, particularly birds.

And so they became quickly acquainted with zoos and wildlife preserves and other such places. But though they carried much wildlife from one end of the earth to the other, there was no sign of her darling bluebird.

A year passed, and another, and another still, and the princess despaired. How was she to find one small bluebird, in all the great wide world, when he had given up all hope of ever being a man, and was not seeking her out in return? She had hoped that, if they did not find him, he would hear rumors of their exploits, and realize who she was, but it had been a vain hope; he thought she was long dead, and had no reason to think she might be a sea captain dealing in the transport of wildlife.

One night, as she sat on the deck staring out at the sea, an otter escaped his cage and came to sit beside her.

"Hello," he said, and the princess jumped, startled.

"I didn't know you were a talking otter."

"I know you did not," he said, "for it is known, far and wide, that you are kind and fair. My owner would not dare to tell you that I can speak, nor the rest of us, just as he would not tell you that the man he has sold us all to is a cruel sorcerer, who will kill us all and use our bones for spells."

The princess frowned. She had not liked the man who'd hired her to carry these thirty assorted creatures, but one could not be a successful businesswoman if one refused to deal with anybody one happened to not get on with.

"We will certainly not be delivering you to the sorcerer, then," she said, for it was true that she was kind and fair. "Is there anywhere in particular you should like to go instead?"

The otter shook his head. "We have been collected all from different parts of the world, and would best like to be freed to make our own ways home."

"Then I shall set you all loose at the first land we come to, for you may do very well just here, but most of your companions are not good swimmers."

The sailors were content enough to free the talking animals, and so they made their way to the nearest port, and there released them all. The others ran quickly away, but the otter lingered.

"I have heard it said," he told the princess, "that you seek a talking bluebird."

"I do."

"Some time ago my former owner attempted to purchase such a creature, but the mermaid who owned him would not part with him for any money in the world."

The princess thanked the otter, and set her ship back into the sea as quickly as possible, for she knew now where to find her beloved, and she was exceedingly angry.

When they were far enough from land that the city by the sea would not be harmed by any storms, the princess stood on the deck and called loudly the name of the mermaid who had once been her dear friend.

The mermaid, who could hear her name anywhere it was said, so long as it was said on the open sea, came quickly. She rose calmly from the still water, and she asked the princess, "Are you ready now to marry my brother?"

"I am not. I am ready to marry my prince, who you have kidnapped."

"It was hardly kidnapping; I bought him from a zoo in a seaside village some time ago. He sits in a gilded cage, which I have enchanted so that he can breathe, and he sings quite prettily for me. I should not like to part with him, but if you married my brother, perhaps I could make him a wedding present. Of course, he would still be only a bird. It has been many years since you abandoned him; I do not think he remembers, now, that he was ever a man. Certainly, he has not spoken a word in many months, but only sings and chirps and eats the seeds I offer him."

The princess, torn between fury and guilt and sorrow, did not speak for several minutes. The mermaid waited patiently for her response. The mermaid could be very patient indeed; she had waited five years now for the princess to marry her brother, and two years for the princess to learn that her prince was in a birdcage under the sea. She knew that if only the princess would finally, finally marry her brother, they would be sisters and dearest friends once more, and all would be well. As for the bluebird prince, she did not much care if he lived or died, but if it pleased the princess for her former lover to live in a cage in her bedroom, and sing her little mer-children to sleep, the mermaid would be kind enough to tolerate this.

The princess thought of the ugly merman, who had saved her from drowning, and who had shouted at the mermaid until she called off her storm. And she told the mermaid, "Very well, then. I will speak to your brother. But you must bring him here, as I cannot abandon my ship until all of the arrangements are made."

The mermaid, confident at last in her victory, went to fetch her brother. The princess went to fetch her sailors, who all armed themselves as best they were able. For if the princess could only lure the mermaid fully onto the ship, which was her own domain, and technically dry land, the mermaid would be able to summon neither friends nor storms, and could be threatened or even tortured until the bluebird prince was safe at home.

The sailors waited below, not wanting to alert the mermaid to their plans. It was over an hour before she returned with her brother, for his magic was not as strong as hers, and he could not travel as quickly. When he saw where they were, and who stood on the ship waiting for him, he heaved a great sigh, for he had thought his sister had finally abandoned this foolish plan.

The princess smiled at him, and waved, for though she still did not wish to marry him, she had remembered him fondly, these last few years; after all, he had saved her life twice.

The merman waved back, and then he turned to his sister, and began to berate her in their language. The two argued, so loudly that it could be heard clearly below deck.

Now it happened that one sailor, a recent addition to their crew, had once loved a mermaid in his wild youth, and had learned her language. It was clear to him, listening to the argument, that the merman had no desire to marry their captain, and was quite fed up with the mermaid.

He went above deck to consult with the princess, and with her permission, called out to the merman that his sister was holding hostage an enchanted prince, who she would not release until they were wed.

The mermaid went white with rage, but before she could react, the merman lifted her and tossed her onto the deck of the ship, where the sailors rushed up to surround her with their weapons.

"Have your brother fetch my bluebird," the princess said, "and promise never to disturb either of us again. And when the bird is safe in my hand I will release you back to the sea."

Foiled, and powerless aboard the ship, the mermaid explained to her brother where to find the bird, with the sailor listening to be sure there was no trick. The merman swam away, and the sailors set up a guard around his sister, and settled in to wait for his return.

The princess was too restless to sit with them, and paced the length of the ship as she waited, ignoring the mermaid the few times she tried to speak to her, as if they were still dear friends. For her beloved was nearly here, but their troubles were not yet over. She had no more idea than she ever had how to break his spell, and if the mermaid spoke the truth, he did not remember that he had ever been anything but a bird.

The sun had risen by the time the merman returned, carefully carrying the cage which was enchanted so that the bird could breathe. As soon as he reached the side of the ship, he moved to unlatch the cage, but the princess cried out to stop him, afraid that if the prince had truly forgotten himself, he would fly away as soon as he was free, and never be seen again.

The sailor explained this to the merman, and he nodded, handing the cage up to the princess. She took it carefully, and allowed her men to release the mermaid. Her brother promised, through the sailor, that they would not trouble the princess again. But as an apology for all the trouble his sister had caused, he gave the princess his name, that she might call on him if her need was great.

The princess thanked him, and as soon as the merman and mermaid had vanished into the sea, she took the birdcage to her room below deck, and carefully opened the little door.

The bird flew about the room in a circle, trilling a happy little song, and then came to rest on her outstretched hand.

"Darling," the princess said. "Darling, I am so sorry it has been so long. Please say that you know me still."

The bird chirped, and made no other answer, but settled more comfortably in her palm. She tried a few more times to speak to him, but it was clear that, though he was quite tame, he knew neither her nor himself.

She did not for a moment entertain the possibility that she had been tricked, or given the wrong bird, for she would know her beloved anywhere. It was surely him, and though he sat now in the palm of her hand, he was utterly lost to her.

The princess despaired. She placed him carefully back in his gilded cage, and went to speak with her crew. For if she could not save him, she must at least return to his brother, and let him know what had happened.

It would be a journey of many months to return to his land, and they had not any cargo to sell when they arrived, but the sailors undertook the trip willingly, for they loved their captain dearly, and were full of sorrow for her.

The princess did her best to lead her crew, but they encouraged her to take time for herself and her mourning, and handled all the work themselves. She spent long hours locked in her room with the bluebird prince, who sang prettily and slept often on her shoulder, and was, as far as she could tell, quite content.

She loved him dearly, and could not forget, no matter how like an average bird he seemed, all that had been between them before. She often told him stories of their time together, hoping to stir some memory, but there was never any sign that he could understand her words at all.

It would be better, she knew, to hand him over to his brother the king, who could arrange a large, sunny room for him to live out the rest of his days, instead of a dank cabin in a little ship. She could return, perhaps, to her own kingdom, which she had not thought of in years, for she had never been close to her parents, before her imprisonment in the island palace. Perhaps her father could set up a happy, sunny room for the bird who had once been a man who had once been her betrothed.

But if she went home, her parents would want her to marry some other prince, and that she could never do. She would never love anyone as she loved the man her bird had been. It was best to take him to his brother. She could continue to captain her ship, and perhaps they could dock in his kingdom once a year or so, and she could go and visit her bird. It would not matter to him—he did not know her. But it mattered very much to her, that she still be able to see whatever was left of him.

If only she had searched harder, when the merman first saved her, if only she had found him before he gave her up for dead, and gave up his own humanity in the process.

He trilled sweetly, and fluttered down to land in her palm, and she cupped her hands around him and wept.

The bird made an indignant sound, ruffling his feathers, as the tears landed on his wings. Above deck, a small storm was brewing, and the princess could hear the distant sound of thunder.

She cried herself to sleep, sitting on the floor, the ship rocking in the wind, the bird safe between her fingers. It was not the first time she had cried over him, but it was the first time she had cried onto him, for the princess had never been told the magic of tears.

When she woke, there was a man lying on the floor beside her. She was so startled by this turn of events that it took her several seconds to recognize her own dear prince, for she had quite given up hope many weeks ago, and besides, she had not seen his true, human face in several long years.

Only mostly certain that she was not dreaming, she shook him frantically awake. He sat up slowly, looking around in a puzzled fashion. At last his eyes fell upon her, and he smiled a slow, unsure smile, for he thought he knew her, but he had long been enchanted, and his mind felt foggy and far away.

With a glad cry, the princess threw herself into his arms, and kissed him again and again, until his long-absent arms and lips remembered their purpose, and he embraced her and returned the kisses.

The princess was weeping again, for joy instead of sorrow, and she knew there were many things to discuss and explain, but she could think of no words but his name, which she said again and again as she kissed him.

At last they were interrupted by one of her sailors, who had come by to discuss breakfast; she was still the best cook by far, but some of the men were learning, and he had come to see whether she was agreeable to oatmeal, which he was fairly confident he could manage.

He was quite surprised to find his captain thus engaged, and would have slipped out quietly to allow her some privacy, but unfortunately her door had a tendency to squeak, and chose that moment to make a most unpleasant sound.

The princess and the prince parted somewhat, startled by the noise, and the sailor stepped hastily backwards, apologizing for the interruption.

The princess waved away his apology, standing and pulling her prince to his feet as well. His legs were weak after so long as a bird, but the princess had become strong in her years as a sea captain, and supported his weight easily.

"Come on, then," she said. "The sea is always beautiful after a storm, and we are nearly back to your brother's city. I will explain everything, and everything will be all right."

And it was, and they both lived happily to the end of their days, riding the seas together. And perhaps the prince was never again quite the man he was before, but the princess was certainly no longer the girl she'd been before her adventures, and they found they still suited each other perfectly.

The Frog Who Married a Prince

Once there was a king who, when he thought he was reaching the end of his life, wished to see his sons married to good women, and his kingdom left in good hands. He had, at this time, three unmarried sons, and as he was an eccentric man, decided that each should choose his bride by archery. Furthermore, he decided that he would leave his kingdom in the hands of whichever son found a bride who could perform most admirably a series of tasks.

The three princes were each instructed to shoot an arrow into the air and follow its course; wherever it landed, there he would find his bride.

"But Father," they asked, "what should happen if an arrow lands nearest to a cow, or a dog, or an abandoned tower? What should happen if the arrow hits a man and kills him?"

"Then you shall marry that cow or dog, that tower or corpse," proclaimed the king, and the princes accepted this, for the doctors had warned them not to cause their father stress in his final days by arguing with him.

The first prince's arrow landed near a noblewoman, and the second's near a merchant's daughter. But the third prince's arrow was caught in a strong breeze and carried far, far away; when at last he found it, he found it held in the mouth of a frog.

Not being the sort of young man to disobey his elderly father, senile though he may be, the third prince got down on one knee and asked the frog to be his wife. The frog accepted, and so he took her to his home, where she hopped happily about, trailing mud wherever she went.

The time came for the brides to begin their tasks. The third prince knew that his frog wife would not perform well, but was not too bothered by this; youngest sons are seldom chosen to inherit kingdoms, even when their fathers make such choices in more traditional manners.

Still, when he went home that night, he told the frog of the task, which was to sew for the king a fine linen shirt.

In the morning, when he was to return to his father's house, the frog presented him with an acorn.

"Here," she said, "I have made you a shirt."

"This is an acorn."

"The shirt is inside," she explained.

"Thank you, darling," the prince said, and patted her slimy frog head, for though no shirt could fit inside an acorn, she was, after all, only a frog, and he was sure she had done her best.

When he reached his father's house, his elder brothers were there already, and each presented the king with a lovely shirt. When the third prince pulled the acorn from his pocket, his brothers could not help but laugh, though they tried to be sympathetic to his plight.

He removed the cap from the acorn, and inside was linen, folded very small; he lifted it up and shook it out, and it was a beautiful shirt made of the softest, finest fabric, unwrinkled despite its journey in the nut.

His father stripped off his own shirt and donned the new one immediately, and the princes were sent home to set for their wives a second task: the baking of an excellent loaf of bread.

The prince went home and asked the frog, "How did you make such a lovely shirt?"

The frog's long tongue shot out to catch a fly. She did not answer the question. He told her of the next day's task, and went to bed. In the morning, she gave him a walnut.

He took this, and thanked her, and patted her slimy head, for she was only a frog, and he was sure she had done her best, though no loaf of bread could be folded to fit inside a walnut.

At his father's house, two lovely loaves of bread were sitting already on the table. He cracked open the walnut, and inside he found a tiny loaf of perfect bread, no larger than the horseflies that were his wife's favorite food. He tipped it carefully out of the walnut, into his hand, and then he set it down on the table.

As soon as it touched the wood of the table, the bread expanded until it was as large as the other two loaves, and all could see that it was far finer than the others.

The prince returned home to his wife, sure by now that she was not merely a simple frog. He tried to question her, but she was soaking in the pool he'd made her, and did not answer.

A few days passed before the final task, which surely even a magical frog could not complete, for each prince was to present his wife to the king at a grand ball, and the king would choose which bride was most impressive, in face and figure, in dress and manner.

The frog was excited for the ball, and he could not bear to tell her how out of place she would surely be, for he loved his frog bride dearly, with her slimy little head and her muddy little feet, and her shining, intelligent eyes.

On the morning of the ball, he woke to find her preparing. She was dressed in a scrap of silk which he thought was a discarded handkerchief, and had found a small cardboard box which would be her carriage, and three mice to pull it along. She was struggling, when he came upon her, to harness the mice, and he knelt down to help, for her frog feet were not meant for such tasks.

"Darling," he said as he tied up the mice, "there will not be room for me in your carriage."

He hoped to convince her, without hurting her feelings, to join him in his own carriage, which was gilded and pulled by fine gray horses. But she was proud of her little box, and determined to make an entrance as his brothers' wives surely would.

The prince went ahead, at his wife's insistence, to his father's house; she would join him there shortly.

At the ball, the prince's brothers teased him, gently, eager though they were to meet his frog bride. The prince himself was filled with dread, for surely the other guests would not love the frog as he did, surely they would mock her cardboard box and her mice, and the handkerchief she wore, and he could not bear to see her hurt, but did not know how to stop it.

There was a great commotion at the door, and the prince rushed out to see, afraid his small wife would be trampled by whoever else might come up the lane.

There was approaching the palace a great carriage of silver and gold, pulled by three white horses, and when it stopped at the gate, there stepped from it a beautiful young woman in ivory silk, trimmed in a pattern which the prince recognized from his handkerchief.

He stepped forward and caught her hands as she came out, and asked her, "Are you my own dear frog?"

"I am," she said, "and by your kindness you have broken the spell that was laid upon me."

And so they went up into the ball together. There was great rejoicing, and when the old king was dead, it was the third prince and his frog bride who ruled, and ruled well.

The Foolish Princess and the Wise Prince

When the prince was born, he was so ugly that the midwife suggested they leave him in the woods to die of exposure. Fortunately, his parents were not terrible people; the prince was kept, and the midwife did not work in that country again. But the queen was filled with sorrow, for though she did not mind having an ugly child, his appearance had already begun to cause him hardship, and he was not yet an hour old.

To cheer her, the prince's godmother said, "I can see that he will grow up to be very wise. And as a gift, to celebrate his birth, I shall give him the ability to grant one person a wisdom equal to his own."

The queen was comforted by this. The prince grew to be a man of great wisdom, whose opinions were sought far and wide, but only by letter, for he was too wise to let his ugliness be often seen. He was a good, kind man, but what good is kindness when one's face strikes fear into the hearts of children?

When the princess was born, she was so beautiful that the attending physician proposed on the spot. Fortunately, her parents were not terrible people, either; the baby was not married, and the doctor did not work in that country again.

The princess' godmother warned her parents, "I can see that she will grow up to be very stupid. You must be careful; it is a dangerous thing to be both lovely and witless."

The king and queen were grieved, and so to cheer them she added, "As a gift, to celebrate her birth, I shall give her the ability to grant one person a beauty equal to her own."

And so it was. But the godmother's warning did not come true; no man sought to take advantage of the lovely, witless princess, for so witless was she, they could hardly bear to be in the same room for long enough to do so. And she saw that she was stupid, so stupid that not even her beauty could combat it, and she was full of sorrow. She was a good, kind woman, but what good is kindness when one has barely the intelligence to stumble through the most simple of conversations?

And it came to pass that the prince and the princess both went one day into the woods, each from a difference direction, to bemoan their fates, for both were lonely and little-loved. There they met. The prince was struck by the beauty and the sadness of the princess. And as for the princess, she was too stupid to see that the prince was ugly.

They told each other, that day, of their sorrows, and being a good, kind man, the prince offered her his birth gift, that she should be as wise as him. In return, he asked that she marry him, but they agreed to put off the wedding for a year, so that she might have time to adjust to the large change he had just wrought in her.

Each returned to their own home, and the princess, when next her parents saw her, was so changed that they hardly knew her. Her old life, her profound foolishness, seemed to her so strange and distant that she could, at times, scarcely remember it, including her meeting with the prince. Suddenly her life was full of handsome men seeking her hand in marriage, and though she was too wise to fall for the charms of those who had been cruel to her, in the time before, there were many new men, as well, and she could not help but be flattered by their attention.

She had never before had to choose a husband and, knowing that it was a monumental decision, was wary of choosing wrongly. She went into the woods one day to consider her options, and it so happened that this day was one year from the day that she had first met the prince. She had not remembered their plan to meet again today, as it was a plan made when she was still so witless.

He was waiting there for her, and she was taken aback at his ugliness, for she had not noticed it before.

He saw her surprise, and said to her, "I can see that you are more aware now of how undesirable I am. You were a different person when our deal was struck, before I had given you my wisdom, and you did not truly understand the agreement we made. I will not hold you to our bargain."

The princess looked at him again, and what she saw was not his ugliness, but his kindness, the way he had cared for her when no other man did. And he saw her look, and had hope.

He told her, for he feared she had forgotten, "If it is only my appearance that disturbs you, it is said you have the power to make me lovely, as I had the power to make you wise."

"Yes," she said, "I do have that power."

Her other suitors forgotten, the princess took the prince home to meet her mother and father, eager to bring together the only three people in her life who had loved her when she was hard to love. And there are those that say the prince she brought home was as lovely as her, changed by her fairy gift. But there are others who say that if he was lovely, it was only to her eyes, for it was not magic but love that changed him. For what good is beauty, when one is kind?

Flash

Photography runs in my family. When Dad died he left me the shop. We sell—sold—cameras of all kinds, and developed film. I was the best in the darkroom. And we have the photo booth, of course, that spits out grainy strips of cheesy couples photos. The money from that, honestly, was the only thing that kept us running, half the time.

I love photos. Theres something wonderful about the way they freeze time, and let it keep on moving, too. Candids are my favorite. Everything just stops, and you can look back, and see how happy it was.

The world is hard. Too big, too fast. It just keeps on moving. With a camera, I can make it all hold still until I get my bearings again. The dark room is the best, though. It's—well, it's dark. Solitary. As long as the light is on, no one will dare come in, and I will be safe.

I used to hide there. I would switch on the light to say I was working, then sit alone on the floor until the world seemed bearable again.

The world is my safe haven now. The gods are fickle, selfish things, short sighted and vain. In their punishments, they have made me a queen.

I have a smile like the sun, and it blinds the world, but it set me free.

Why a goddess might walk into a camera shop is beyond me. It is a strange world we live in. Why I would flip, after developing them, through her photos, knowing what she was, is a better question, though one I can answer, at least.

I do not live outside my dark room. I do not leave my shop. Not alone. Only when there is the camera to separate me from the world. All of the life I see, I see through a camera—my own, before I take the picture, or someone else's, as I develop the images. Everyone wants to live. We must snatch the life we can.

And oh, what life a goddess must have to share.

Everyone knows them, even a no one like me, from the tabloids and the magazines. Other cameras have been drawn toward their power, too. And everyone knows that they are always having affairs. It is the way of the gods, and not for us to judge. Why should it matter, then, that I saw in shiny black and white which of the others then held her heart?

She was angry.

If I was so fond, she said, of the frozen moments stolen from someone else, then I should have those moments, and only those, forever.

I am a camera with legs and a soul.

The first time I blinked, and the man at the counter froze like a photo, I was only afraid. But the second time, I felt so safe. The whole world, I saw, could be as still as a photograph.

I live now in the dark room at night, and no one shops here, but I hardly need them—I have not learned to undo the magic, and with the fear of becoming a sculpture, people deliver, happily, all that I need. One brave foolish soul is posted every day to watch if I leave my lair, but they never clear the streets fast enough, and my artwork decorates the town.

There's nothing to fear now. She gave me control.

It can be lonely, perhaps, but I live as I always have, through candids, secondhand.

The boy walks in backward, which will not help him, but I am intrigued enough to press together my lips and lower my eyes. He is sixteen at most, and swerves past the happy family immortalized at the door.

"I have a girlfriend," he tells me, faced carefully away, "and her stepfather hurts her."

He asks what price he can pay, and the world comes abruptly to life again, a photo shop full sized. I stop the world to protect myself, but never thought it could protect someone else.

I decided long ago to be the villain, if that is what keeps my world dark and empty and bearable, but if it comes with money, well, I can do this one good thing. I trust him enough to offer my hand, and blindfolded follow him through the streets of this ghost town that is mine. In a moment now I will flash, and click, and see.

The Man With the Silver Nose

What makes it funny is that I loved him.

"Only you," my daddy would say if he was here still, "could fall in love with a serial killer." But he isn't here, so I say it to myself.

I was eight years old when he first rode into the city in his mourning-black carriage, here because he couldn't bear to live in the land where he lost her. His wife fell to the same wasting sickness that took his nose, right cheekbone, and left leg below the knee, all replaced with shining silver prosthetics. He must have been over forty then; forty was an old man, when I was eight. (Not as old as my grandfather, who was still alive in those days, and by far the most distinguished person I'd ever met at that time—Grandpa had been a pirate in his youth, and had a tarnished silver hook to show for it. These prosthetics were ever so much more elegant.)

I was ten when he remarried, and eleven when his new wife, the daughter of a local merchant, died in a shooting accident on the spring hunt. When I was fourteen he began courting my oldest sister.

He'd gone gray by then, and his hair shined to match his face. I had just begun to have what my mother called Feelings, with a capital F you could hear, and I had all my Feelings for him. He was elegant. Distinguished. Not like the silly boys who came to our house before.

My sister preferred the silly boys, but my brother's doctors preferred to be paid, and he was her only suitor with money.

She married him before I turned fifteen, and died before I turned seventeen, in the same dreadful illness, we thought, that took Daddy and my brother and a quarter of the city.

He was in our home often, after, to share in our mourning, and I flirted with a reckless abandon built of raging hormones and a deep,

deep sadness. When the mourning period was over, he proposed to my next oldest sister, and she accepted.

She died in childbirth, along with the baby.

By the time he married me, I was twenty one to his fifty five, proud of myself despite being older than I should have been for a first marriage. I'd had no other offers, but I'd gotten the one husband I wanted.

I would rather have had my sisters alive, of course. And I didn't expect him to love me. He was wealthy; we were not. My oldest sister was beautiful and kind, and I thought he had loved her—marrying her little sisters would be his way of continuing to support her family.

He wore mourning black, always. He had enough to mourn, I suppose—four wives, an unborn child, half a leg, and a bit of his face. I started wearing black in solidarity the day he proposed. It was no great loss; color never suited me.

He laughed, and called me his little mourning dove.

After our wedding, he took me back to his manor, up to his bedchambers, and sat heavily on the bed.

"Time, then, my little dove, to see what kind of monster you've married."

He rolled his trouser leg up to remove his silver leg, then reached behind his ear to unhook the facial prosthetic. Beneath the false nose and cheek was bone and inflamed tissue, with snot filling any empty space between. I did not think until years later that the kind of monster he meant might be something deeper within; I thought he meant only his face, and I loved his face, with all its missing pieces.

I reached out to touch what remained of his cheek bone, and he flinched back—I should have asked first. Exposed bone must be painful.

"I'm sorry," I said. "I don't mind it."

He stared at me for a long moment.

"All right, then." He refastened his leg and stood. "Let's get you to your bedchambers."

"Aren't we going to—I mean, shouldn't I stay with you?"

"There'll be time enough for that; it's been a long day, and we both need rest."

"Oh." I'd never been with a man, and was more curious than eager, but as long as a marriage was unconsummated it could be annulled. And I had waited so long to be his wife.

"Tomorrow night," he told me, and kissed me on the cheek.

He was different, the next morning; he had always been kind and gentle with me, but he was kinder, gentler, in the morning. He treated me like a fragile, precious thing, and my love for him only grew. We kept our own bedchambers, but visited each other often, though more often to talk than anything else. He was a good husband, when he was there, which admittedly was not often—all of his business was still in his old land, where he had lost his first wife, and he went back often to handle things.

I missed him so badly, those long weeks he was gone. My mother did not like to visit, and the rest of my family was dead. I spent most of my time wandering our manor. He did not—you must know this—he did not try to trap or trick me. I know the stories say he tried. Perhaps he did, for the others. Perhaps the others had not looked at the snotty hole in his face and said "I do not mind it;" my sisters, certainly, would have minded.

He never moved a new wife into an old one's bedroom; the rooms of the three wives he'd taken since moving here sat empty, as well as the half-finished nursery of the child that would have been my niece or nephew. (I wanted so badly to have a child of my own, to fill our achingly empty home with joy and laughter and mess, but no child ever came. A blessing, I suppose.) I spent many long hours sitting in the dusty rooms that had belonged to my sisters, when my husband was not home. He did not seem to mind this; we had mourned them together, years ago.

I did not discover the one locked room in our home until we had been married for nearly five years. It was a large house, and this was a small room in a back hallway, near the servants' quarters. I had thought it was a linen closet, which was why it seemed so odd to find it locked.

My husband returned home a few days after, and stayed for some months, and the locked door was forgotten for a time.

But when I asked him about the little closet in the back hallway with the locked door, his eyes moved to the left, and he tapped his silver cheek, and he told me, "It is nothing, just an old cupboard I have not bothered opening since I moved in."

The eyes, the tap on the cheek—it had been five years of marriage, and I had known him for years before that. I had seen him lie before, but I'd never seen him lie to me.

He never gave me a key. I know the stories say he gave me a key. But my brother had been a troublemaker, before he died, and he had taught me to pick locks when I was a child. The next time my husband left town, I picked the only lock in our house, and inside the little closet I found the corpses.

I had not seen my sisters' bodies when they died, but it had never occurred to me to doubt that they were in the wooden boxes we buried. It had never occurred to me that they might be, instead, in a linen closet in the home of the husband we shared.

There were six bodies. Two were just barely recognizable, still, as my sisters. One must have been the merchant's daughter he'd married when he first came to town, though I had never known her well enough to identify which set of remains was hers. The other three women—I don't know. I still don't know; they were never identified. No local women had gone missing since he came to town. Perhaps he brought the bodies here from his old city.

I closed the door and relocked it. I went about my usual business, and when he came home I greeted him gladly.

He was home for eight weeks, and in that time I tried not to think of the bodies. I loved him. I had loved him since I was little more than a child. He was everything I had ever wanted.

He was a serial killer who kept his victims in our closet.

I do not know, looking back, why I was so certain, so quickly, that he had killed them, that he was not merely keeping their bodies in some morbid memorial. But I was quite certain, and the coroner's report, later, proved me right.

On the last night that he was home, I lifted the prosthetic gently from his face, and cleaned out the snot from the hole where his nose had been, as had been my habit since a few weeks after our marriage;

it was hard for him to do it himself, to look in the mirror at what his face had become.

(I wonder if he told me the truth, about how he lost his leg and cheek and nose, about how he lost his first wife. I wonder if she even was his first wife, with more corpses in the closet unaccounted for.)

I cleaned his face and the prosthetic both, and set it carefully aside, and I kissed him, careful to avoid the exposed bone, still tender after so many years. It was a good night.

In the morning I saw him off as I always had, and took a few hours to prepare myself. And in the early afternoon, I picked the lock on the closet again, and I stood in the open door and screamed.

It all happened very quickly after that. The servants came running, the constable was called, and I was taken home to my mother. I believe my husband was arrested a few hours after reaching his destination, when the news had reached the local sheriff. I did not see him again. I was not asked to attend his trial, only to write a statement which someone else would read aloud; this was, I gather, to spare my delicate feelings.

I returned to my childhood bedroom, as much a tomb now as my sisters' bedrooms, in my husband's house. I sat in my room and wept.

My mother believed that I wept for my sisters, or for fear of the fate which could have been mine; I allowed her to believe this.

I wept for a husband I loved, for our life together which was over.

And when I was finished weeping I laughed. Only I could fall in love with a serial killer.

The Kiss and the Frog

The frog considered the girl. The girl considered the frog.

"Look," she said at last. "It's not—I mean, no offence, but no. I think I've been pretty cool about this, but you gotta draw the line somewhere. And I'm drawing it here."

"But you said—"

"I don't care what I said. I ain't getting in bed with a damn bullfrog."

She winced as she said it. Her ain'ts only slipped out when she was agitated. Her damns, too. All those words she wasn't supposed to say, seeing as how she was a proper young lady, now. The frog had produced three ain'ts so far, which had to be some kind of record. The frog was very quickly becoming the bane of her existence, and it had only been four hours.

"You owe me," the frog said. "I retrieved your golden ball, which otherwise would have been lost forever."

"Okay, first of all, it was yellow. Second, I was up to my knees in swamp to get it back myself by the time you showed up. And I got it for a buck fifty at the grocery store last week—it's not like it was some irreplaceable treasure."

The frog frowned. Well, she thought he frowned. It could be hard to read facial expressions on frogs.

"You agreed you owed me a favor."

"That was before I knew you were a perv," she countered.

"I am not a perv."

"Then what are you wanting in bed with me?"

"The logistics of that idea—" The frog shuddered. "Just to sleep."

The girl thought this over. "Still won't work. You're tiny, and I'm a restless sleeper. I'd roll over and crush you."

It would be a shame to crush a talking frog, especially if he wasn't a perv. Enchanted frogs were probably an endangered species—she'd never seen one before.

"Oh," said the frog. "Perhaps you could kiss me?"

"What was that about you not being a perv?"

"It doesn't have to be with tongue or anything."

"Well, I should hope not. You eat flies with that thing."

"All right," he said. "All right. Maybe you could throw me at the wall, then?"

"What? No! How is killing you deliberately better than crushing you in my sleep?"

"You are giving me nothing to work with here! It's bed sharing, kissing, or throwing me against the wall. You have to pick one!"

"Why?"

"So I can stop being a frog!"

"You're an enchanted frog?"

The frog nodded. The girl shook her head.

"Magic ain't real." Damn, there went the ain'ts again.

"I'm a talking frog," he said flatly.

"Okay. Well. You make a good point."

"So can we get to breaking the spell?"

The girl took some time to consider her options. "A kiss," she decided. "It's gross, but a lot less likely to result in me cleaning frog guts off of anything. But you're gonna have to rinse your mouth out first."

She poured a small amount of mouthwash into the bottle-cap, and waited politely outside the bathroom while he gargled and spit. This was—there was an enchanted frog on her bathroom counter. She was going to kiss an enchanted frog.

He wouldn't be a frog anymore once she kissed him. That— that was—was he going to turn into a prince? Was she going to have to marry him? She didn't want to be a princess; she was still trying to get the hang of this "proper young lady" thing.

No, he couldn't be a prince. What would a prince be doing in Illinois? She would have heard on the news, too, if any princes had gone missing from Europe or wherever.

The frog came hopping out of the bathroom, smelling more like mint and less like swamp.

"That really wasn't necessary," he said. "I don't think you have to kiss me on the lips."

"You don't even have lips. But this is a weird situation, and the mouthwash makes me feel better."

She closed her eyes and kissed the frog. When she opened them there was a naked man sitting on her bedroom floor. She said several extremely unladylike words.

"Sorry," he said. She grabbed the blanket off her bed and tossed it over him.

"I'm gonna raid my dad's closet," she told him.

He lifted his head from under the blanket, face red, hair wild. "Thanks," he said. "For, you know. De-frogging me."

"Your vocab has seriously chilled in the last few minutes."

"Yeah, well, I was trying to be in character, but you didn't seem to like it."

"In character?"

"When you've spent as much time being an enchanted frog as I have, you put a lot of thought into what an enchanted frog sounds like. Fancy. Like something out of an old book."

"You sounded like a jerk. Next time just open with the fact you're under a spell."

She went to the closet. Her dad was bigger than him, but she didn't exactly have a lot of spare men's clothes lying around. She picked out some of the smallest stuff he had, and left the frog alone in her room to change.

They needed—they needed a plan. Dad was working late tonight, but her stepmom would be home soon. Her stepmom was pretty cool, concerns about her language and her dad's cholesterol aside, but a strange boy in her bedroom, in her dad's clothes, would probably stretch the limits of her coolness.

"So," she said when he opened the door, holding up the pants with one hand. "Can I call you a cab or something?"

"You in a big hurry to get rid of me?"

Yes, she thought.

"No," she said. "I just—if you've been an enchanted frog for a long time, your family must be worried about you."

He shrugged, which made the neck of her dad's shirt slide down past his shoulder. "Don't have one."

"Oh. Sorry."

They stood there for a moment in awkward silence.

"Sorry," she said again. "I've never—I don't really know anything about, like, post-spell-breaking etiquette."

"Well, I think traditionally we'd get married and I'd take you home to my palace. But that seems—a bit premature. And I don't have a palace. So."

"So," she echoed. Another awkward silence.

They heard the front door swing open.

"Damn it. We're out of time. I should have waited to kiss you until she got home—there's no way she'll believe you used to be a talking frog."

"What do we do?"

"You'll have to climb out the window. There's an old treehouse at the edge of the swamp—you must have seen it. I'll meet you there when I can."

The boy who had been a frog made his way to the treehouse, and the girl made her way to the front door.

"I've been thinking," he said when she joined him at the treehouse. "And I think I can live here, if you don't mind, and I can get a job at the steel mill, and buy clothes that fit me. And maybe when I'm finished with work each day, you could come and visit me?"

"That is an extremely unromantic plan for an enchanted frog."

"Well, I didn't ask to be an enchanted frog, did I? I'm very sick of magic, and a steel mill sounds like a nice practical place to work."

And so the frog went to work at the steel mill. And when he could afford clothing that fit, and later an apartment of his own, he went to meet the girl's parents, who were quite taken with him. The frog and the girl did get married, after all, though it took them ten years, and they never lived in a palace, but instead in a sensible little manufactured home at the edge of the swamp. It is not, perhaps, a very romantic ending for an enchanted frog, but as he was thoroughly sick of magic, and she thoroughly uninterested in being a princess, or even a proper young lady, it suited them both quite well.

King Lindorm

Once there was a King, who had so lovely a Queen. At last they had a wedding, and when they went to bed the first night, there was nothing written on their wedding sheets; but when they stood up, it stood there written, that they should have no children together. The King hereover was highly grieved, but the Queen more: she shook, it was so hard that they should have no heir to their Kingdom. One day she went out in deep thought and came then to a remote place. There she met an old woman, who asked if she would tell her what was wrong; the Queen looked up and answered: "Now, it cannot help anything to tell you: this is a thing you cannot help me in."

"Now, it might even happen that I could," said the old woman, and asked if she would only say what was wrong.

Yes, she could easily say it: and she told her, how it stood written on the bed of their wedding night, that they should have no children, and it was for that she was now so sad.

She could give her counsel enough, said the old woman: then she might have children. In the evening, as the sun went down, she should take a Rovs (a drinking cup with two handles) and leave it in the northwest corner of the garden; in the morning, when the sun rose up, she should take it up again. Then there would stand two roses under it, one red and one white. Should she take the red and eat it, then it would be a boy; should she take the white, then it would be a girl; but she must not take them both.

The Queen came home and did as the old woman had said. In the morning, the sun rose up, and so she went into the garden and took the Rovs up, and there stood two roses: one red and one white. Now she knew not which one she should take and eat: if she took the red, and it was a boy, then he might go to war and be defeated, and so she might as well have had no children. She thought she would take the white, so it would be a girl, and she could stay home with them until she was married and went to another Kingdom. So she took the white and ate it. It tasted so very good that she took the red and ate it too. She thought to herself: so she would have twins, and did not think any farther.

Now it came to pass that the King was at war, and when the Queen noticed that she was with child, she wrote to him and let him know, whereover he was much pleased. And now it was in the fullness of time that she should give birth to a Lindorm. As soon as he was born, he dug himself under the bed in her chamber, and there he had his home. There he stayed, and a letter came from the King, saying that he would be home in a short time. And the time came for the King to come home, and he was driving his carriage up to the Palace. The Queen went out to receive him, and the Lindorm also went out to greet the King. He jumped up beside the coach and said, "Welcome home, Father!"

"What!" said the King, "am I your father?"

"Yes; if you do not wish to be my father, I shall split both you and the castle apart."

So he had to accept it after all. They went in, and the Queen had to make her explanation of what had come to pass with the old woman and herself.

A few days later, the whole council and all the nobles were summoned, and welcomed the King home and celebrated his victory over all his enemies. The Lindorm came also and said: "Now I will be married, Father!"

"Yes, and who do you think will have you?" said the King.

"If you do not get me a wife, whether young or old, whether big or small, whether rich or poor; then I shall split both you and the castle apart."

The King wrote out to all the kingdoms, if any would have the King's son. So there came so very lovely a princess; it seemed so strange to her that she should never look to see who she would have, until she should enter the hall they would be married in. Then came the Lindorm and stood at her side. The wedding day was over, and they went into the room with each other. As soon as he came in with her, he split her apart.

There it was, and it was the King's birthday some time after. Then when they all sat at the table, the Lindorm came again and said, "Now I will be married, Father!"

The King said: "Who do you think will have you now?"

"If you do not get me a wife, whether young or old, whether big or small, whether rich or poor: I shall split both you and the castle apart."

The King wrote to many kingdoms, to ask if any would have the King's son. There came again so very lovely a princess from afar. She did not see the groom until she came into the hall they were married in. Then came the Lindorm and stood at her side. But when the wedding day was over, and they came into the room with each other, the Lindorm split her apart also.

Some time after that, it was the Queen's birthday. Then the Lindorm came in; he came to sit at the table and again he said: "Now I will be married, Father!"

"Now I cannot give you more wives," said the King. "Now two mighty Kings make war against me, whose daughters I have given you for wives, and what shall I do with them?"

"Let them come! So long as you have me, they must come, even if there are ten, but if you do not get me a wife, whether young or old, whether big or small, whether rich or poor: so shall I split both you and the castle apart."

The King was made to promise it, but he was much distressed. There was now an old man, who was a shepherd for the King. He had a small house in the woods, and he also had a daughter. The King went out to him and said: "Listen, good man! Will you not let me wed your daughter to my son?"

"Oh no, that I cannot do, for I have only one child, to support me in my old age. For another thing, if he will not spare so lovely a princess, so he will not spare my daughter, and so I think it is a sin."

But the King would have her, and the old man was made to give his consent.

The old shepherd went home and told this to his daughter. She was very sad and went through the woods in deep thought. As she went, there came an old woman also through the forest, and she would pluck berries and apples. She was in a blue skirt and a red vest.

"What is it that you are so sad for?" she said.

"I can easily have reason to be sad, but it cannot help to tell you this, for it is not something you can help me in."

"Oh, it might even happen," said the old woman, "if only you will tell me!"

"Yes, it is such: I must have the King's son, and it is a Lindorm; he has split two princesses apart, and now I know that he will also split me apart."

"Oh, there could well be a solution to this, if you will obey me," said the old woman.

Yes, she would obey her.

"Now when you have stood before the priest with him, and you know you will enter the chamber, then you shall wear ten gowns; and if you do not have them, then you must borrow them. Then you must demand a tub full of lye and a tub full of sweet milk, and as many whips as a fellow can carry in his arms, and these must be put into the chamber. As soon as the Lindorm gets there, he will say: Fair Maiden, cast off a gown! Then you shall say: King Lindorm, cast off a skin! So he shall say such to you and you to him, until you get to the ninth gown and him to the ninth skin: then he will have no more, but you shall be in one gown. Then you must take hold of him, when he is nothing but a hunk of bloody flesh; then you shall dip the whips in the lye and whip him as long as you think he can bear it; then you shall put him in the sweet milk after, and then you shall wrap him in the nine gowns and lay him in your arms; and then you shall go to sleep, if only for a little while."

She thanked her for the good advice, but she was afraid nonetheless: it was a great risk to take with so cruel a beast.

The wedding day came, and there came a coach so big and so magnificent; there were two ladies in it who were to dress her as the most beautiful bride. She came up through the King's Guard and into the hall, the Lindorm came in and stood behind her, and they were married. It was drawing to night, and they were going to the bridal bed. So she demanded a tub full of lye and a tub full of sweet milk and whips there. The men did laugh at it; it was peasant

nonsense and fancies, but the King said what she asked for she
should have, and so she did. Before she went into the chamber, she
put on the nine gowns, as well as the one she was in. Then they
came into the chamber, and the Lindorm said: "Fair maiden, cast off
a gown!"

So she said, "King Lindorm, cast off a skin!"

And so it was, until she came to the ninth gown, and he to the
ninth skin; and then she grasped the whips, for by then he lay on the
ground, and could hardly move, and the blood ran from him. So she
took the whips and dipped them in lye and whipped him, as strongly
as she could, and for so long, so there were bits and pieces stuck to
the whips; so she bathed him in the sweet milk, and she wrapped
him in the nine gowns. And so she went to the bed and took him in
her arms. At last she fell asleep, but it was late. When she woke again,
she lay in the arms of a beautiful prince.

Morning came, and no one dared to look in the bridal door, for
they were afraid it was with her as with the others. Then the King
wanted to go and look inside. This time as he opened the bridal door
she said, "Come right in! All is well here."

He came in and was so glad, he fetched the Queen and all the
others; and there was such a celebration over the wedding bed. They
got up and came into another chamber and got dressed; for their
chamber looked bad. Then the wedding was held again with joy and
pleasure, and the King and Queen held her so dear: they never knew
the good they would do her, because she had saved their son.

The Tailor and the Queen

I met the queen of Ilefrisa when I was seventeen, and I loved her the moment I saw her. Of course nothing is ever that easy, and I was no one, a travelling merchant, a tailor, a step above a pauper, maybe two. And she was rich and proud and beautiful, and I knew she had to have me.

I offered to make her a dress, the finest dress the world had ever seen, to wear at the wedding of her brother in the next kingdom over. A real, honest dress, not like that business with the emperor last year. The queen was perfect, and she deserved something better, something real. Something better than me, certainly, but I meant to offer myself to her, all the same.

She accepted the offer of the dress, though I had not yet dared to offer her myself. It was not until the dress was finished and all laced up around her that she asked me the price.

"Only that you take me as your escort to the ball where you wear this dress."

The queen did not wear my dress to her brother's wedding. Nor did she wear it to the next ball, although she did let me design that one as well, and I accepted money for it. We had a deal, the queen and I, that she would not wear the finest dress in all the world until she went out with me in her company.

I knew from the beginning how long I would wait. But surely it would be worth it. I wooed her with ball gowns and sashes and elaborate head dresses, with dainty golden shoes, and cloaks, and everything she asked for. I designed the curtains and the couch covers in her sitting room. With every dress I stitched I told her how I loved her, and she never answered.

We played card games in her sitting room. We played chess in my sewing room, and abandoned the rules quickly, for I could never keep track of them. I was always the pawn, in the games we played, and she was my queen.

She was always my queen.

I thought that she was fond of me, at least. She was so strong and proud in public. When I laced up her dresses she giggled, and she yelled at me sometimes, seldom serious, but she yelled and laughed, and even just her smallest smiles were something incredible. She was always so calm and cold in public, often kind, but so utterly unflappable.

I flapped her. It was a start, surely, that I could flap her.

I was court tailor for years. I saw others court her, of course. Great grand dukes and counts and knights and princes. She never saw any kings—they would only detract from her own power, and of course that would never do. She was so strong.

Somehow I never thought they would have her. Oh, perhaps I would not have her, either. I was not nearly worthy of her. But none of them had ever made her smile. She always smiled at my dresses. I paid very little attention to the surrounding politics. All I knew was that my queen was untouchable.

And it was for this reason that I was so surprised the day she walked into my workroom, in one of the finest everyday gowns I had created for her the year before, smiling nervously, clenching and unclenching her hands in the fabric at her sides. Her smiles were never nervous. She never clenched her hands, and she would never wrinkle fabric this way. Not my fabric.

"What can I do for you, my Queen?"

"I know that we had a deal, concerning that first gown."

I nodded slowly, thinking, foolishly, that perhaps my time had finally come.

"And I am so grateful for all you have done for me since that time. But I was hoping that perhaps we might make a new deal, that perhaps you might allow me to wear the dress to my own wedding."

She smiled again, even more nervously this time, and it occurred to me that I had not seen her so much in recent weeks. She must have been occupied with this new suitor. This new suitor that she was going to marry, instead of me.

"Of course you'll have to design a very fine suit for yourself," she went on, "and be presented to the court before the wedding ceremony, as the finest tailor the whole wide world."

I nodded again, and tried to smile. She only ever talked like that for me, with alliterations like the whole wide world.

I wondered if her husband-to-be had seen her nervous smile. I wondered if he had heard her alliterations.

Selfishly, I hoped he hadn't, and generously, I permitted her to wear my dress. It still fit perfectly—she had not grown a hair in all of these long years.

I had no desire to be presented to the court, especially on this, the saddest day of my life, but she insisted, and I had never been able to deny anything to my queen, not since the deal for the finest dress was first struck. I left her to her suitor for many days, and began to create my suit. She did not seek me out, and I told myself that it was all for the best, anyway, that she would never have been able to choose me, a tailor, even had she wanted to, and that she should never have to be alone.

She sent maids to tell me all the plans. She did not ask me to design her husband's suit. I tried to make a habit of not caring—it was all over, anyway. A married queen could not play chess in the tailor's quarters. It was hardly appropriate for an unmarried one to do so.

I never even bothered to ask the name of the groom. It was nothing to me. I would be gone, I supposed, when the wedding was over, off to offer my services in some other kingdom.

Perhaps she had heard of the trick I pulled on the emperor. Perhaps that was why she did not ask me to dress the groom. Perhaps she knew I would be jealous—I hoped she knew I would be jealous—and thought it unwise to put me, with the history I had, in charge of something so very important.

I would not have ruined her wedding that way. I loved her far too much to do so, strong though the inclination to humiliate her intended might be.

The court was all gathered, the music all playing, when finally a girl was sent to drag me from my chambers. I would rather not have seen these particular festivities.

The queen dashed over to see me, utterly undignified. Her happiness, then, could be set free by someone besides myself. This man had pulled off her mask not only in private, but in front of the entire court.

Good. He was better for her than me, then, in every possible way. She could be happy, as she deserved.

"Finally," she said, slipping her hands into mine as she had never done before. "You're dreadfully late, you know."

She was incredible, in all the wedding finery, made for another wedding so long ago. In all the years since then I had never made a better gown, although it was the queen herself, I thought, that made it truly wonderful.

"I hardly think I matter much, in the midst of all of these festivities."

"Of course you do. Yu matter more than anyone else here. Except for myself, perhaps."

"And what about your groom?"

"My groom? I'm marrying you, darling."

She had been tugging me slowly across the room. I stopped abruptly, and she leaned closer, peering anxiously into my face.

"That is, if you'll have me, of course. Though it would be embarrassing to call things off so very late as this."

"You don't think perhaps you should have told me who you were marrying?"

"It was meant to be a surprise. You love surprises. Like that horse I got you in the fall. And you don't think I buy horses for just anyone, do you?"

"Why?"

"You never pay attention to anything, all locked up in your room with your fabrics and threads. The city has been a nightmare for weeks. And you are absolutely marvelous, and haven't a drop of noble blood in you, and there's a history, already, of tension with the emperor. We're on the brink of revolt, you know. Marrying you is the boldest political move I could make."

"So it's all about the politics, is it?"

"Well, that and that I love you, of course."

"Of course. And now I wish I'd made myself a finer suit."

Dreams Remembered

Long, long ago, in the days when dreams walked among us, there lived a Prince. This Prince was named Felan, and at the time our story starts, he has just returned home, after an absence of many months.

It had been a spell of some sort that had drawn him away, a wicked sorceress or a deal gone awry. He was puzzled by the details, as he was by many things since his return. There seemed to be something missing.

He had stumbled to the palace gates in rags—that much he remembered—and had nearly been turned away before he thought to present his seal ring. Then there had been much rejoicing, for the King and the Queen had long believed him dead, and after he had visited the barber and the tailor and the royal baths, there had been a grand ball, as well.

The King and Queen had asked many times to hear of his adventure, and he had been quite surprised to find that he hardly remembered it. They had assured him that immediately after his return, before he even embraced them, he had promised them many great tales. He was quite surprised to find he could not remember this, as well, and returned to his chambers troubled, and they did not speak of his absence again.

He threw himself into the duties of princehood, as a distraction from this hole in himself, and within a month had half forgotten that there was something he had forgotten.

A doctor had been summoned once, though the King and Queen had attempted to conceal the reason for his visit. Felan had seen though this, and had let himself be examined nonetheless, and the doctor had declared him perfectly fit. If the King and Queen still worried, they did so in silence.

In the day, he lived as princes do, and thought not of his lost adventure. At night he dreamed.

The first dream came a fortnight after his return, and was only of an ogre, looming hideous above him, speaking words he did not know. A sennight after that he saw a weeping girl.

Perhaps they were memories, perhaps only dreams. His parents had all but accepted his unexplainable return; it did not seem prudent to stir their hopes with what may be only fancies.

In the third dream he saw that the girl had no face, though her dress was of gold and her tears were of silver, and this loss cast shadows on his waking for many days. In the fourth dream he saw that the ogre was but the scum on a pond, and determined to brush him away, and reveal the beauty hidden beneath. But when he lifted his sword, it became a pick axe of the finest crystal, and suddenly he stood in a vast forest. For many nights he dreamed this dream.

In the fall he slew a dragon, and when he slept that night he dreamt the entire forest had become kindling, and the girl stood before him, smiling. For a moment her face sharpened into perfect clarity, before the dream was swallowed by the mouth of day, and the image faded in the sunlight.

In the winter he did much paperwork, and dreamed always of sorting seeds, and did not see the girl or the ogre.

A year passed, and another, and the time came for Felan to marry. During the day, for many days, he read of all the princesses to be had, and sorted through the portraits their fathers had sent. The dreams were one thing, but it would be good to have a real, flesh and blood woman. At night he tried to clear the pond scum with a spoon, the ogre looming behind him. He thought that he was searching for the face of the girl, but found instead that he was trying to sort through all the fish in the seas.

On the night after he had chosen a bride, he dreamt of his mother, crossing the empty hall to meet him. But when she took his hands, he saw that she was a much younger woman than his mother, and dressed in wedding finery. When she kissed his cheek, she became the ogre, and he woke alone in the darkness.

He did not dream again.

Preparations were made, and Felan was very busy, and had half forgotten, by the night before the wedding, that he had ever dreamt at all.

The faceless girl wept, that night, ceaselessly, and he woke with a heart twisted in knots, knowing that her name was Cathleen, and that he had lost her forever.

But she was merely a dream, and he had his wedding to attend. He met the bride, and she was as lovely as a summer day, far superior to the portraits he'd seen, and certainly not an ogre. But before the ceremony could begin, their party was invaded by a peasant girl.

She was not so tall as Felan's bride, nor so slender, and her hair was not as fair, nor her skin as clear. Throughout the disorder, as the King and the Queen demanded to know who she was and from whence she had come, she looked only at him, with a terrible sadness in her eyes.

"Felan," she said, "do you not remember me?"

He did not.

"Foolish boy. You did not obey my instructions." And she kissed him, and his vision was cleared, and he saw his dream.

"Cathleen."

"I am not so beautiful as the wife you could have this day. And I have no dowry, since you have slain my father, and I have lived in a hovel these past two years."

"I have dreamed of you," he said. "In a dream you are better than any woman of flesh and blood, and in waking I can only apologize, for I disobeyed you and allowed the ogre's final spell to take hold."

"I am here, she told him, "and flesh and blood as I always was, and if I can forgive you for the trees and the seeds and the fish, and for killing my father, who was my father, though he was an ogre too, then I can forgive you this, as well."

And so they were married, and the stories of Felan's absence, once remembered, were told throughout the land, and the bride he had chosen was married to his younger brother. And they all lived, until the end of their days, quite as happily as anyone could expect.

The Marquis of Carabas

There was, of course, a cat. Was it a talking cat? Perhaps. Cats can do many impressive things, if they only put their minds to it.

Was it a cat wearing boots? Certainly not. For all cats have quite strong feelings on the subject of fashion, feelings which can be summed up as, "Perhaps it's all right for humans and the occasional dog, but it should all be kept far, far away from me." They feel this pertains most especially to any fashion going over the feet, which are meant to be wild and naked and free, for the purposes of scratching and climbing and clawing at things.

He was a quite lovely cat, but not the sort to sit still and let himself be petted. The princess first encountered this cat when she was taking a short ride in her least elegant carriage; he ran suddenly in front of her, spooking the horses, and she went around the front to calm them, and to see that the cat had not been trampled.

When she reached out to touch the cat, it leapt up and went racing through the trees, and she followed it to where there was a small pond, and a young man standing in it, soaking wet and naked to his waist, which was as much of him as was not still underwater.

"Hello," said the naked man.

"Hello," said the princess.

"I'm terribly sorry to be—only, you see, my clothes have been stolen."

"I'll fetch you a blanket from my carriage," the princess offered, and after a brief pause she curtsied; just because a man was naked in a pond in the woods was no reason to be impolite.

She introduced herself, when the man was wrapped up in the blanket and dripping onto the mossy ground. She waited several seconds for the man to introduce himself, as well, which he did not do. The cat butted his head into the man's ankle, and he stood a little straighter.

"Sorry," he said. "I'm, um, a marquis. The Marquis of—of Carabas."

The princess had always paid very good attention in geography class, and was quite certain there was no such place as Carabas. Also, he mispronounced "marquis."

But he was a very handsome young man, and he had a very lovely cat, so she did not call him out on the lie.

"I don't suppose you have anything else to change into nearby?" she asked instead.

The marquis shook his head. "Carabas is—well." He looked down at his cat, staring at it for what seemed a very long time. "Carabas is not, er, it's not terribly far from here, of course, but I think my horse must have run off—yes, definitely my horse ran off, stolen by the clothes-thief, I suppose. I could make the walk in— um, in a few hours, but it wouldn't be terribly pleasant, barefoot and naked and soaking wet."

"I suppose you'd best come home with me, then," said the princess. "I did see a shirt and some trousers, behind a rock over there, but surely such cheap, worn clothing would be little better than the blanket, for so distinguished a person as a marquis."

She pronounced the word correctly, and he turned a deep, deep red, which she felt shifted his face from classically handsome to rather adorable.

"Come along, then," she said. "There's plenty of room for you and the cat in my carriage. It's a shame about your horse, though. I'll be sure to have someone keep an eye out for it, and in the meantime I suppose you'd best borrow one from my father's stables to make your way home to Carabas."

When he was clean and dry and dressed in her father's clothes, the princess took the marquis to the stables, where it quickly became clear that he had never mounted a horse in his life.

"It's just that we use a very different style of saddle in Carabas," he explained, as the princess valiantly suppressed her laughter.

She nodded as solemnly as she could manage. "New saddles can be tricky. But my father is rather a collector of international riding techniques. We have just every style of saddle and bridle and stirrup you could imagine, in a shed over that way. Perhaps we could find you something more familiar?"

The young man went quite pale, and she swallowed another giggle.

"Really, I shouldn't like to trouble you so. Now that I have clean clothes, and these very sturdy boots, I should be able to walk home myself."

"Nonsense. A marquis should never have to lower himself to going on foot."

She did manage to get him up onto the horse, eventually, and after a moment of consideration, buckled the cat into a saddlebag. He scratched at her, and made a noise of profound disgust.

"Off you go, then," she said, dropping the reins and swatting at the horse to get it moving. "It was ever so lovely to meet you."

The horse galloped away, his rider clinging desperately to his neck, his imprisoned cat howling, and finally, the princess allowed herself to laugh. Her father would forgive the loss of a horse and a nice suit, when he heard how much fun she'd had today.

~

She had not expected to see the marquis again, but did, quite often, always accompanied by his cat. The cat did not seem to hold a grudge about the saddlebag, and often twined itself about her legs and purred, though it did not much like to be petted.

The cat and the marquis met her father, who found them just as delightful as she did. They were dreadful liars, yes, but it was the dreadfulness of the lies that made them so amusing. It was all a great deal of fun, in fact, until the marquis invited her, rather nervously, to visit his home.

"In Carabas?" she asked.

He nodded.

"I would love to," the princess said, very much looking forward to seeing how this latest lie would play out. And so they rode together in her carriage, as riding horses still made the marquis quite nervous.

They stopped in front of the wicked ogre's castle, which everyone knows is a foolish place to stop.

"This—um. This is my home. Welcome to Carabas?"

This—this was ogres. Ogres were not to be joked about. "Your home was occupied, last I heard, by a very deadly, man-eating ogre."

"An ogre?" the marquis repeated.

The princess nodded.

"But my cat is in there!" he cried. He jumped out of the carriage and ran toward the entrance of the castle.

"Oh dear," the princess said quietly. She was quite fond of her ridiculous liar, and of his cat as well. Could she bear to just sit here in her gilded carriage, knowing they were both being eaten just inside?

"Very well, then," she said to her horses. "In I go."

The castle was a dark, dank place, with far too many human bones lying about for comfort. Not, she supposed, that any quantity of human bones at all would be comfortable. The exact quantity of human bones that should be lying about in hallways was zero.

She had not got very far at all when she heard a great and terrifying roar—the sort of sound, she thought, that an ogre might make if his home were invaded, or perhaps if he were scratched by a very darling cat who certainly did not deserve to be eaten. She broke into a run.

She reached the great hall, terribly out of breath, to find her marquis looking pale and bewildered, and his little cat pouncing on quite the smallest mouse she'd ever seen. He killed the thing and took it to a corner to eat, looking terribly pleased with himself, while the princess caught her breath.

"I've defeated the ogre," the marquis said, sounding a bit unsure of himself.

"Really? It's not one of your ridiculous lies?" One couldn't take chances with ogres.

"What lies?" he asked, indignant, and she began to laugh, feeling rather hysterical.

He reached out cautiously to place a hand on her shoulder, and she did her best to compose herself.

"Well, it was Puss that did it, really. But anyway, the ogre's defeated. And, er, now that the intruder is gone, perhaps I could show you around my home?"

"How long, exactly, has this intruder been here?" the princess asked. She knew already that the answer was forty years, at least, but was interested, as always, to see what he might come up with.

"Oh, ages really," he said. And then, perhaps remembering that he had known nothing about the ogre when they first stopped the carriage, "I'd say an hour, at least."

"An hour," she repeated, glancing at the bones and rubbish strewn about the room, and the cobwebs filling every corner.

"He's a very messy houseguest."

"Certainly. Well, it's your castle now, anyway—that's only fair, if you defeated the ogre. Perhaps we could find you a title, too."

"I already have a title! I'm the marquis of—"

"Of Carabas, yes, I know. But darling, there's no such place. Did you really think a princess wouldn't know her geography? We're hardly ten miles from my home; I would certainly know all about any marquis who lived here."

"Oh."

"It's quite all right, though. You can be a marquis if you like, or a duke, or a prince. I suppose you'll be king eventually, but if you're quite stuck on being a marquis, you could always stay a consort."

He looked thoroughly baffled. It was an adorable look on him, but then, most looks were. "Why would I be king?"

"Darling," she said again. "Honestly, don't you know anything? If you defeat the ogre, you get to marry the princess. And that, of course, is me."

He continued looking baffled.

"I suppose, if you really don't want to marry me—"

"No," he said. "No. I mean, yes. That is, I do. Want to. Only I didn't know about the ogre—I guess ogres don't bother about eating things as boring as miller's sons."

"Well, I happen to find miller's sons quite interesting. Certainly more interesting than marquises. Marquises, I've always found, are

just dreadfully boring. That was how I knew you couldn't be one,
even if you had known how to pronounce it."

He blushed and she allowed herself, finally, finally to kiss him,
while the cat twined around their ankles, purring furiously.

Violet and Zorzal

"That was a lovely performance," said the king. "In return, I'm going to let you marry my daughter."

The minstrel went pale. "You can't—I mean, um, that is, usually, sir—uh, Sire—usually people give me some pocket change."

"I'm afraid I don't carry money."

"Then consider the song a gift," the minstrel said, sounding a little desperate.

"Nonsense," said the king. "I'll fetch the priest."

He left them there, his daughter on her velvet throne, the minstrel on the floor, lute in his lap.

Her father had said—she'd known he was angry. But she hadn't thought he'd meant it when he promised to marry her to the next beggar that came to their door.

There was still time. Maybe he hadn't—maybe he would come back in a few minutes without the priest, and it all would have been a bad joke.

There was a horrible feeling in the pit of her stomach that told her it wasn't.

Violet studied her husband-to-be, who was carefully tuning his instrument, and wouldn't meet her eyes. He was drab, for a minstrel. Usually even the poorest of musicians patched their worn clothes in bright colors. This one was brown—brown hair, brown skin, brown cap, brown shirt, brown trousers, brown boots, brown satchel at his back. The only hint of color was in his lute, wooden, but painted in much-chipped gold.

She didn't even know his name.

It all happened very fast when her father came back. Within a half hour, she and her still-unnamed husband were leaving through the back door, which she'd never used—never even seen—all her remaining possessions stuffed into a small leather sack.

Her new husband had not yet said a word to her. It was dark, and beginning to be cold. Her slippers were not made for walking— why had she not thought to change them, in the last few minutes she had in her rooms?—and her feet were sore, though they had not gone far. She did not know when or where the minstrel planned to stop; she was afraid to ask him.

Finally, finally, he turned off the street—were these her streets? Was this her city? She had thought she knew her home well, but all of this was unfamiliar, everything from the back door on. Dark, dirty alleys, anxious, frowning faces, people dressed in rags, people sitting filthy on the sides of roads—sights she'd never seen, and never expected to, in her father's city.

Finally he turned off the street, and knocked on the door of a small, dilapidated building. He rummaged through his pockets, and offered a small handful of copper coins to the man who opened the door.

They were taken into the building, and into a room barely large enough for the bed it held, which was half the size of Violet's bed at home.

She sank into the tiny bed, miserable and terrified and exhausted, and thought she would sleep immediately. The minstrel did not lay down beside her; she heard the door swing shut, and looked up to find him gone.

She did not think a beggar would have the money for two rooms in even such a run-down inn as this, but didn't have the energy to find him and ask.

Sleep did not come as easily as she'd expected. The mattress wasn't down; she thought it might be straw. She had heard that poorer people slept on straw. There was no glass in the window, only a sagging, crooked shutter, which banged in the slightest breeze.

She woke in the morning to find a strange man in bed beside her—her husband, of course. Her husband.

She was trapped between his sleeping body and the wall, nervous to disturb him, so she took the time to study the man she would spend the rest of her life with. Dark and drab. Foreign, she thought. There had been a bit of an accent when he spoke last night, as well as the skin tone. The only person she had left in the world, and she'd only known him a few hours, didn't even know his name.

She didn't understand. What had happened last night—her father wasn't a cruel man. They'd been at odds, these last few years, as she refused to be married to any candidate he could produce, but he—he was her father. He'd raised her.

Oh, she'd had nannies and tutors and governesses, of course. But it was her father who showed her how to write out her name, who set her carefully on the back of her first small pony, who taught her to dance, when she was still small enough to stand on his shoes, by carrying her, giggling, through the steps, again and again until she knew them on her own two feet.

She had not wanted to marry at all, and if she must marry, had wanted to marry someone who loved her, or at least saw more in her than her dowry and her father's allegiance. But more than any of that, she had not wanted to leave her home. Her home, where she had a father who loved her, and cousins who loved her, and aunts and uncles. Her home, where the councilors and couriers and servants had watched her grow up from a child, where she knew each palace guard and maidservant, each hunting hound and horse, by name.

Some small, foolish part of her had hoped that if she could only put things off for long enough, her father would give up on it all, or one of her cousins would grow bored of youthful indiscretions and consent to marry her. Or maybe there would only be less important people left to choose from. One of her father's knights, perhaps. Someone who would be honored to stay in the palace with her, instead of whisking her away to his own lands.

And now she had found a very unimportant person indeed, and still she was being whisked away, because her father didn't love her anymore.

She did not want to cry, not here, not now, when it might wake this man who wanted her no more than she wanted him, when he might be angry with her for it, or when he might feel an awkward sort of pity she didn't know how to handle.

But Violet had never had good control over her emotions; it was another large part of the reason she'd turned away so many suitors, anger or embarrassment flaring at innocuous comments they'd made. She wept despite herself, and more loudly than she would have liked, and it woke him, of course.

His back was to her; she saw him begin to sit up, then pause, stiffening, before he laid back down. They were going to pretend, then, that he was still asleep, that he didn't hear her crying.

She found she liked that option no better than the others, and composed herself as quickly as she could, waiting until she was sure her voice would come out steady to ask him, "What is your name?"

He sat up then, and turned to face her on the too-small bed. "Zorzal," he said.

He left the bed, making room for her to do the same, and she went to sit on the edge. They—they would need a plan. She didn't know how to be a beggar's wife, didn't really know how beggars lived, save some vague idea that the reality was significantly less romantic than what she'd seen in storybooks.

"Do you have enough money for a second night here?" she asked. She doubted it; he had rummaged through his pockets for some time before producing the coins he'd given the innkeeper.

Zorzal shook his head. "Your bag—what did you pack last night?"

Violet stood, pulling on the slippers she'd cast off last night before doing anything else. The floor was filthy.

Her bag was where she'd dropped it last night; she opened it and dumped the contents onto the bed. She'd only had a few minutes, after the priest was done, to pack up her entire life. Her life, which filled a suite of rooms larger than this whole inn, cut down to a single bag.

She'd changed out of her gown. There had been a ball last night, a ball where she was supposed to have chosen her husband, and she was still in the ballgown when the beggar—when Zorzal—came. She'd changed into one of her everyday dresses, then stuffed two more in the sack she'd found at the back of her wardrobe, and a nightgown. Three dresses seemed too little, but she didn't have space to spare for more.

She'd left behind her crown and signet ring, but had packed a pearl necklace and a ruby broach, knowing she could never wear them again, thinking they must be worth more money that her new husband could make with his lute. She'd packed her plainest cloak and her favorite book, and that had filled the space available. She'd paused on her way out the door—the last time she would ever step through this door—to grab a handful of ribbons she'd pulled out of her hair and dropped on the ground after dinner the night before.

Zorzal looked over her shoulder at the mess of all her remaining possessions.

"I suppose we could sell the jewelry," he said after a moment.

Violet nodded.

"Of course, no one will believe I didn't steal it, someone like me. The necklace we can break, sell one pearl at a time to different shops. It won't be for long."

"What won't?"

"This—this marriage. Your father will regret it in a few days and come looking for you. Probably have me executed if he thinks I've touched you."

"He wouldn't execute you," Violet said. She wouldn't let herself believe he would come back for her; she would never have believed him capable of doing what he'd done last night. Her father had become a stranger, and she would not give herself false hope for him.

"I didn't plan to stay in this city long. But it will be harder for him to find us if we move."

"Good. If he has regrets, let him work to correct them."

"You want to leave?"

"Yes," Violet said. She didn't want to, really, but she didn't want to be here, either. She would never be home again; what did it matter where else she went?

At least in some other city, she would be less likely to be seen by someone who might recognize her as a disgraced former princess.

They left their small room, both still dressed in their clothes from the night before—Violet was not sure he had other clothes—

and Zorzal led her to a long, wooden table, old, rough, and sure to produce many splinters. At the table they were served small bowls of thin, sour porridge with unidentified lumps of something floating on top.

"Eat it," Zorzal advised her quietly. "It comes with the room; I don't know when we'll eat again."

After breakfast, they each took their own bag, and Violet followed Zorzal as he carried out whatever errands he felt necessary before leaving town. He didn't explain himself to her. He stopped several times to ask for directions, further cementing her assumption that he was not from here. She thought of being annoyed that he did not ask her for directions, but it seemed she did not know her own home as well as she'd thought; every road they turned down was unfamiliar.

He broke off a pearl from her necklace, and traded it for a few silver coins, which he traded to someone else for a larger number of copper coins. The copper coins were exchanged for a loaf of bread, a bit of dried meat, sturdy boots for Violet, and finally, a seat on the back of a small, dirty cart headed south, with just enough space for the two of them between several large, foul-smelling crates.

"Where are we going?" she asked him.

"Esrania. My mother held a small property there. I think the house is still standing, and empty. I doubt you're well suited for a life on the road."

Violet was too tired to be offended by something that was probably true. The king of Esrania was one of the men she'd turned down last night; she was too tired to care about that, either. That king had been friendlier than most, more interested in her as a person. He had been her father's last great hope for her marriage, and she had rejected him cruelly, in a fit of rage. A mistake—he'd doubtless have made a better husband than a minstrel beggar would, even one who owned some property several countries away.

She had been so angry last night. She had been angry for so much of the last three years, as suitor after suitor after suitor demanded things she wasn't willing to give, as her father pressured her to make an allegiance that would strengthen their kingdom. It was all gone now.

She sat in the back of the cart, strewn with straw that did little to soften the jostling caused by bumps in the road, and stared at the tallest turrets of her lost home, until they disappeared into the rising fog.

She thought of all the things she had lost. She would never again go to the stables with a basket of carrots for her favorite horses. She would never be scolded by the seamstress for wearing through the elbows of her velvet dress. She and Thomas and Joseph would never again convince the music master to play that song when their cousin Peter came in to dinner late. She would never again pick clumsily at the piano keys, for her father insisted her lessons continue, though she had no musical talent.

She would never gather in a giggly huddle with all her ladies after a ball, they would never take down each other's hair and loosen each other's stays and gossip late into the night. Her cousin Joseph and her lady Maria were besotted with each other, though neither would admit it, and she would never tease either of them again.

She would not take long, slow walks around the courtyard with her beloved but outgrown childhood pony. She would not work on great tapestries to be given as wedding gifts to relatives and allies, would not learn the clever stitches that her aunts had mastered, would not notice a dropped stitch from earlier in the day, and have to unravel three perfect, beautiful lines to fix it, and what a strange thing that was to mourn.

She would not argue with her father about whether she should have a new dress for the next party, or reuse an old one, each of them taking a different side in the argument depending on the purpose and guest list of the event. She would not see her father again at all, would not give him his birthday present, lying half-finished in her wardrobe.

And what should it matter, if he had his present or not, when he had cast her out before she could finish it? What did it matter, the long hours she had worked on it, these last few months, what did any of it matter, why should anything matter at all? She had nothing. She was alone.

The anger was gone. She was only empty.

It began to rain; she dug the cloak out of her pack to stave off the worst of it. The cloak was over-large, and after a moment she remembered her new husband, and lifted the edge for him to huddle under as well. He scooted closer to fit, looking surprised.

The cloak did little to protect from the heavy rain. Already soaked through, Violet could not say when it was that she started crying again.

"I'm sorry," Zorzal said.

"It's not your fault. You had no more say in this than I did."

He didn't answer.

~

"Princess."

Violet woke slowly, soaked and sore and shivering. The rain had stopped, the cart had stopped, and night had fallen.

"We'll need a room for the night," Zorzal said. "I won't make you sleep in the open after the ride we've just had, but it'll take another pearl."

"Why didn't you exchange them all at once?" she asked.

"Less suspicious to have one pearl than a string of them, and pearls aren't so heavy as coins to carry. I don't want to sell more than one pearl in any city. And only in the big cities. Our situation is bad enough as it is—heaven knows what will happen to you in the real world if I'm thrown in prison for stealing fine jewelry."

It took too long to sell the pearl and find an inn; Violet needed badly to be out of her wet clothing. But then, all the other clothing she owned was in a bag that had also been out in the rain. It was likely not much drier.

When they found an inn, Zorzal stood outside the door of their room while Violet changed quickly into the driest dress, at the very bottom of her pack. It was a little damp, but still a relief after what she had been wearing. They swapped places so that Zorzal could change as well, into a second drab, brown outfit; she felt odd and showy beside him, in her soft blue dress.

"We can't waste the money for a second room," he told her when they were both in dry—well, drier—clothes.

"I know."

She sat on the edge of the bed. The mattress was still straw, and the window still un-paned, but at least there was room here on either side of the bed, so she would not be trapped against the wall again. She began sorting through the damp contents of her bag. Zorzal used the blanket on the bed to carefully wipe his lute dry, then pulled the loaf of bread from his bag. He tore off a piece and handed it to her; it was the first food she'd eaten since their unappealing breakfast, and she didn't even care that it was damp.

Her book was only a little wet. The pages would wrinkle, but she did not think any ink had run. She wondered absently if Zorzal could read—many musicians could, but then she had seldom dealt closely with musicians that were also beggars. Probably she should become better acquainted with the man she would spend her life with; they had barely spoken.

"Why are you here, begging, when you own property in another country?"

"It was my mother's home, years ago; I've never lived there. It's small, rundown, no real land attached. I like the life I live. I like travelling, seeing new places. And it's not—begging isn't—well, I offer a service in exchange, don't I?"

"I could travel with you," Violet offered, not really meaning it—she couldn't imagine spending the rest of her life like this, bumpy roads and lumpy beds and nothing steady or familiar.

"I don't think you could."

"I'm sorry my father did this to you."

He shook his head. "I still think he'll change his mind. But if he doesn't...better that you're here with me. I won't—won't take advantage, or hurt you in any way I can help. I think many things about this life may be a hurt for you, who have lived so differently, but I will spare you what pain I can. He could have given you to anyone—I like to think that I am a good person, at least."

They spread their few belongings across the limited floor space to dry, and Violet looked over the small sad collection of everything they owned. Zorzal had his cap, his lute, and only two sets of clothing — the soaked set and the one he was wearing. Not even any nightclothes. Half the loaf of bread remained, and the dried meat. She was still very hungry, but painfully aware that she was now very poor; she would have to rely on Zorzal, who had experience with poverty, to decide when and how much they could afford to eat.

She woke alone in their room. Zorzal was gone, both of their bags were repacked and sitting near the door, and there was a bit of dried meat on Zorzal's empty half of the bed.

Violet ate it, noting the grease stain it left behind on the bedsheets; she wasn't sure how difficult such a stain would be to remove, or whether the innkeeper would charge them more for damages—so many things she'd never had to consider before.

She didn't know what had become of her husband, but was fairly certain he would return, for his things if not for her. She waited for him there, nervous to venture into the rest of the inn, unsure what she would say if anyone asked her questions about her journey, or her husband, or her too-elegant clothing.

"I've arranged another cart for us," Zorzal said as soon as he walked into the room. "Leaves in a half hour. We can take it all day—it's going in the right direction—but there'll be other passengers joining later."

They spoke little over the course of the morning. Zorzal made conversation with the cart's driver, and largely ignored Violet, which suited her well. She had no idea what to say to her new husband, could not begin to imagine what their life together would look like. She was afraid, and becoming more so as the shock of the last few days wore off. Zorzal had called himself a good person, and she was inclined to believe him—his life had been destroyed as surely as hers, and yet he had not been unkind. But he was still a stranger, taking her to a strange land, which was exactly the fate she had worked so many years to avoid.

They had reached a small town by midday, and Violet and Zorzal remained in the cart, eating their now-stale bread, while the cart driver disappeared down the dirt road in the center of town. He returned with the other passengers Zorzal had promised, which were pigs.

Violet had never seen a live pig; she expected a foul smell, but was unprepared for the size. She'd seen them roasted, whole, on a banquet table. But those were wild boars, naturally larger than farm animals, and still dwarfed by everything else a proper feast entailed.

She hadn't expected a standard pink pig from a farm to be so large it could trample her with ease. She moved to the front corner of the cart, as far from the three pigs as she could get. Zorzal laughed at her, and she ignored him and tried not to be angry; she could not afford to lose her temper on this man, and told herself he likely thought she was disgusted, rather than afraid. She could not let herself think she was married to a man who would knowingly laugh at her fear.

They separated from the cart and the pigs near nightfall, in a tiny town with a tiny inn, where Zorzal got them a tiny room. The bed filled all the space save a strip of wall just wide enough for the door to open, and it was too narrow for them both to lie in without being pressed tightly together.

"There's no other room available," Zorzal told her, "even if we could afford it."

"It's fine."

It wasn't. She slept that night sitting up, back against the wall, arms wrapped around her legs. She didn't know how Zorzal slept; he was sitting on the edge of the bed, tuning his lute, as she fell asleep, and he was gone again when she woke, although this time he returned within a few minutes.

There was porridge served in the main room of the inn, and it was the best food she'd had since leaving home.

She was so sick of being hungry, and afraid it was just beginning.

They rode in a cart all day again, and her whole body was stiff and achy, from the lack of activity and the bumps in the road both. They were joined in the late morning by three men, and the cart did not stop until night fell.

The driver pulled the cart to the side of the road; there was no sign of any village nearby.

"We're stopping here?" Violet asked, though it was obvious that they were.

"It'll be fine, Princess. You'll sleep in worse places before this is over."

If any of the men thought it was strange he called her princess, they didn't react.

She wasn't looking forward to sleeping in a rough wooden cart out in the open air, but more worrying was the fact that she would be alone, miles away from anyone else, with essentially five strange men—the three passengers, the driver, and Zorzal himself, who she had only known for less than a week.

She lay pressed tightly against the side of the cart, Zorzal too close for comfort in the small space, but separating her, at least, from the other men. It was a long, sleepless night, spent staring up at the starry sky and wondering how different the constellations would be when they reached their destination.

Even her sky would be changing.

She dozed through the morning as the cart kept moving, unsure why it felt safer to sleep with the same strangers in the day than it had at night.

~

The next several days were much the same. She became badly bruised from days of being jostled about in various carts, there was never enough food, and their supply of pearls became ever-smaller. Towns were fewer and farther between as they travelled, and Violet convinced Zorzal to cover less distance each day if it meant sleeping in an inn that night. She knew that this was costing them more money, but could not bring herself to care; that night surrounded by strangers beneath the stars had been terrifying.

One day their cart stopped for lunch in a field in a farming village, where two long lines of wooden benches had been set up. It was good when they could eat in a group of people, like this or when they had breakfasts in an inn; the food was better, and there was more of it, than whatever Zorzal found for them.

The sun was shining brightly, and she pulled the hood of her cloak up over her head as they sat on one of the benches. Zorzal frowned.

"You look ridiculous. I bought you that cheap dress in the last town so you would stop wearing that damn cloak everywhere."

She had been wearing the cloak partly to hide her too-elegant dresses, though it was true that the cloak stood out nearly as badly, at least in this weather. It had been the height of summer when she left home, and would only get warmer as they continued to travel south. But her dresses were not the only reason she wore the cloak.

"A coarse linen dress cannot protect me from sunburn."

"Oh," he said.

He would not have thought, of course, of sunburn; he was darker than her, from a hotter, sunnier climate, and likely used to spending all day every day beneath the sun, if the life they were living now was the life he'd always led.

He pulled the hood of her cloak down, and replaced it with his own cap. It was too large, slipping down toward her eyes, and his hair, uncovered, was a tangled mess. She folded her cloak and put it away, feeling oddly pleased.

They had to switch carts after lunch, as the one they'd taken this morning was moving now in a more easterly direction. Their fellow passengers for the afternoon were a small family—a young husband and wife and their daughter. The woman tried to engage Violet in conversation, but she wasn't sure what she was allowed to talk about, and tried to deflect most of her questions to Zorzal.

He talked easily with the husband and wife, one arm slung around Violet's shoulders, and called her "Princess" in a casual way that made it feel like a pet name.

It was a long afternoon, and the young girl on board began quickly to complain of boredom. It was the first time Violet had travelled with a child, and she found she much preferred her to the farm hands who were their usual companions; the girl was small and precious and very correct about the tedious nature of their ride.

Violet convinced Zorzal to play the lute; he had tuned it, but had not properly played since the song that won him her unwanted hand in marriage. He pulled out his instrument reluctantly, but the child, whose name was Rosa, was delighted with it, and the music kept them all occupied for many hours.

She had forgotten how beautiful his playing was. He played primarily songs for children, today, and she had never before considered such music lovely, but coming from his fingers it was.

They were all songs familiar to Rosa and her parents, and most of them Violet remembered from her own childhood. They all sang along, even the cart driver joining in occasionally. It was the happiest day she'd had since leaving home.

It was two days before they reached another city of any size; Zorzal told her they had passed from her country into the next, and it would be some time before they reached another long stretch of farmland.

They had spent another night in a cart, but this cart had two drivers, who slept in shifts, and they had travelled through the night. The sun was just rising as they reached the city where the cart was to leave them.

The first thing they did in the city was sell two of the pearls, to two different men several streets apart. One paid significantly more than the other.

"The pearls were identical," Violet said, after he'd accepted a smaller sum from the second man.

"Less money means fewer questions. There wasn't a second man in this city who would have paid so much."

"Then you should have sold both pearls to the first man, or saved the second for another city."

"You've an endless rope of pearls, Princess, and each one puts us in more danger should someone notice."

"We cannot live forever on my jewelry, even if you were more discerning in your sales."

"No," Zorzal agreed, "we cannot. Here, give me my cap."

She obeyed reluctantly, conscious that her hair was flat and tangled beneath it. It had been weeks now since she'd washed it— just one of many disadvantages to being a beggar's wife. But Zorzal smiled at her, and reached over to smooth down her hair. He dropped the cap on the ground, pulled out his lute, and started a jig.

Every time someone dropped a coin in the hat, he turned to look at her, eyes wide, as if the money were a beautiful surprise.

When the cap was heavy with coins, he picked it up, and poured all the money into the small leather pouch where he had been keeping all the coins her pearls had earned. He placed the cap carefully back on Violet's head, then took her hand and pulled her along, weaving his way through crowds, up and down streets and in and out of shops, buying what he felt they needed.

There was still money in the pouch, though not much, by the time they found themselves in an inn, in a room with a bed large enough, at least, that she needn't touch Zorzal in the night. He emptied both of their bags, packed now with everything he'd bought.

Violet looked over their purchases, spread out on the lumpy bed. She picked up a small knife, sharp and bright and new, with a smooth wooden handle.

"And what do we need this for?"

"You'll recall we're travelling with pearls and rubies."

"So the knife is for stabbing burglars."

He shrugged. "Of course, you're the biggest risk of all, I suppose. Travelling with a princess. Of all the crazy things—I wonder how much the ransom would be, if someone found out and kidnapped you."

"Nothing. No one wants me."

"Of course they do, Princess. You don't think your father would come running, if he got your little finger and a ransom note in the post?"

"Oh. Ew."

"Well?"

"I think he'd care. But then I thought he wouldn't really marry me to you, too."

"It'll all work out, Princess. And mostly the knife is for shaving. I've lost my old one, and I don't fancy a beard in the summer heat. Here, let's pack up the food—the inn serves supper."

~

She didn't think about his kidnapping comment again until over a week later, when they reached an inn in a small town, full of men she'd tentatively labeled as bandits, based on the memories of illustrations in childhood reading material.

They didn't look as if they suspected the truth, even though Zorzal continued to address her as "Princess." But they did look, just in general. At her, in a dress that was beginning to wear a bit thin, and at Zorzal, carrying a valuable instrument on his back, his arm around her waist, significantly smaller than any of them.

Maybe it would have been better if she'd been wearing his hat at the time. It was clearly a man's hat, and too large for her. People could be expected to stare, with her dressed like that.

She didn't like the places their eyes travelled to. Places far from where her hat would have been sitting. Zorzal, still exuberant from a street performance minutes earlier, didn't seem to notice. He left her in the dining hall, alone with several large men in the far right corner, while he went to handle things concerning their room. She stood near the wall, clutching her bag and reminding herself that appearances could be deceiving.

Some of the worst suitors she'd ever met had looked absolutely charming.

One of the men in the corner approached her as soon as Zorzal was gone. "So, Princess. And where does a girl get a name like that?"

Violet quickly decided that she didn't like the man. "Um, my— Zorzal."

"Ah, yes. The princess and the songbird." He looked over at the rest of the group. "We could have some fun with that, couldn't we, boys?"

"I don't—" He reached forward and brushed her hair back. "I don't understand." She was beginning to be afraid, though. So much for deceiving appearances.

His hand trailed down the side of her face. She was frozen. "Please..."

"No." The man withdrew his hand to turn to the speaker. Zorzal, in the doorway, looking lethal. He wasn't so small, really, she saw. Well, he was, but a compact, muscular smallness. He was looking, now, as if he could hold his own.

"Good," the man said. "We're all here, then. The princess and the songbird." She wished he'd stop calling them that.

"No," said Zorzal again. "We don't do this. You don't touch her." The man laughed and stepped forward. Violet started to edge away.

"Violet. Go outside. We're not staying here." She ran, dropping her bag as she did so, and waited on the street for what felt like an eternity before he followed, with her bag, his lute, and the beginnings of a black eye.

He pushed her hair back, an echo of what the man had done, oddly comforting where it had been terrifying before. "Are you all right?"

"I'm fine. Your eye—"

"It doesn't matter. Nothing matters. We'll have to walk through the night, though. We're not staying in this town."

"But why—what did they want?" She was determined not to understand.

"Let's just go. I'm sorry, Princess."

They walked for nearly an hour, through the pitch-black night. Zorzal kept on looking anxiously over at her, at least when it was light enough to see. She assumed he continued to do so in the darkness. He asked three more times if she was all right, and apologized several times more.

"Well, I'm tired," she told him the third time he asked. He was practically begging her to complain about something. "Are we really going to walk all through the night?"

"That town wasn't safe anymore. It'll be hours before we reach another."

"But couldn't we just sleep here?"

"On the side of the road? I'm sure that's much safer than what was supposed to be a respectable inn in a respectable town."

"I'm sorry."

"No. I wish we could stop. I didn't want you to—I didn't want to make you—and I know you hate sleeping in the open."

"What if we went to the other side of that hill there? We'd be out of sight of the road. It would be fine."

"You really want to sleep on the ground, Princess?"

"It must be better than not sleeping at all."

"All right. I'm sorry. Yes, we can do that. The foot of the hill. That one there?"

~

Violet woke on the damp ground, Zorzal's nearness to her more comfortable here in the morning chill than in a narrow bed.

She sat up slowly; Zorzal made a soft noise beside her, then woke as well.

"Violet," he said.

It was the first time he'd used her given name when they were not in a state of panic. He was a musician, and he spoke it like a song, drawing out all three syllables. Vi-o-let, not Vi-let.

"It's early," he said. "Go back to sleep."

She did; the ground was uncomfortable, but last night had been awful and draining.

She woke again to Zorzal, touching her gently on the head, calling her "Princess."

"Time to get up?" she asked. She felt stiff, and her dress was damp from the ground.

He nodded. "We've a long walk ahead."

"I'm sorry," she said, not quite sure what she was apologizing for. It was all so much, it had been too much since the night they met, but last night—last night—

Zorzal rolled over and stroked her hair again. "All right, Princess, don't cry. It's all right. I'm sorry, too. You shouldn't have to worry about this. You shouldn't have to be here at all."

"Not your fault," she murmured. It was quiet for a long moment, as she tried to compose herself and he continued to run his hand through her hair.

"Right," he said, finally. "He'd just have married you to someone else if I hadn't come. Not my fault. And there are worse options out there, aren't there?"

138

"Definitely." She sat up slowly, a little reluctant to dislodge his hand. "We'd better start walking."

~

They walked every day for the next week—Zorzal had developed an aversion to strangers. Violet understood the reaction, and worried about his eye, and didn't complain about all the hard walking. Zorzal, on the other hand, seemed to suddenly crave complaints, asking constantly if she was all right, and if she wanted to stop and rest. He told her his eye was fine, and she caught him staring at her guiltily, anxiously, several times, although he was the only one to come through the ordeal with even the slightest damage.

They stopped in small towns and at small farmhouses to buy food and to sleep. There were no more performances. Mostly they walked in silence. Violet attempted several times to engage Zorzal in conversation without much success; she had no idea what the two of them had in common that they might talk about.

She told him a thousand times that she was fine, and wavered between appreciation for and irritation at his sudden careful attention. He started using chairs or tables or wardrobes to block their door at night. She worried that he wasn't sleeping much. He worried about everything imaginable.

One night they walked well into the night, and there was no town.

"I miscalculated the distance," Zorzal admitted, when it had been fully dark for over an hour.

"Another night on the ground, then," Violet said, trying to sound more cheerful than she felt.

She woke up before him that morning. He was asleep sitting up, leaning against a tree, clutching his lute, and she suspected he had not meant to sleep at all.

She sat there and waited for him to wake on his own; there was no reason to rush things. When he started to move around she leaned forward to look down at him.

"Zorzal."

He smiled up at her, clearly not yet fully awake. "Yes, Princess?"

"Say my name." He frowned, and she leaned forward farther, so that her hair, loose and tangled, brushed against his face. "Zorzal."

"Violet." He said it slowly, pronouncing every syllable, just as he had before, and she lowered herself until they were almost touching, then rolled over to lie on the ground.

"I've decided I like sleeping outside."

Zorzal sat up "Good. Are you all right?"

"I am wonderful, except that I am very sick of you asking that, and I am very badly in need of a bath."

~

In the next town large enough to have one, Zorzal bought her a trip to the public bath house.

It was much more public than she had anticipated, and she began to wish he hadn't sent her inside alone.

But on the other hand, why should it be any less awkward for Zorzal to see her naked than only a group of strange women she'd never have to meet again?

Of course, he was her husband. He should, in theory, see her naked at some point in their lives.

Not if her father was coming back for her, though. If he was going to do it, she wished he would just get it over with. Wondering was—she thought wondering was worse than knowing for certain she would never see him again.

A woman in the bath house helped her to brush out and braid her hair, and then presented her with a well-made homespun dress she'd never seen before.

Zorzal had gotten her new clothing while she'd washed.

He dropped his hat back on her head when she emerged, and asked, "It fits?"

She nodded, and he smiled and put an arm around her waist.

They walked to the next town before nightfall, since it was only a few miles, and Zorzal arranged a ride for them for the morning—

the first ride they'd had in many days, though he wouldn't let her out of his sight while he arranged it.

"I'm sorry," he told her that night, just as he was drifting off. "This won't be forever. You'll have something better soon."

She fingered the hem of her new dress, and thought that this was good enough for now.

~

Violet did not know how long they spent travelling; she would estimate it at several months. It was long enough for Zorzal to become accustomed to using her given name, and for Violet to become accustomed to sharing a bed, often quite small, with a man who was no longer a stranger.

He taught her his favorite songs; she had a strong, clear voice, and began sometimes harmonizing during his performances. (It turned out she had some small musical talent after all—her father should have let her sing, instead of setting her to half a dozen instruments she'd never mastered.) The book she had brought along was full of fairy stories, and she took to reading them aloud when they rode in carts, to make the time pass more quickly. They walked nearly as often as they rode, until Violet grew to love it, cutting through woods and across fields instead of always following a road, stopping to look at anything interesting they saw. She grew fond of his cap on her head, and his arms around her shoulders, and thought less and less of home.

"We'll cross the border into Esrania sometime tomorrow," Zorzal told her as they prepared for bed in a small room they'd rented above a pub one night, in a village too small for a proper inn.

"We're nearly done, then," she said, and the thought was bittersweet.

"Another week, at least, but I think no more than two."

Violet nodded; they lay down side-by-side in the bed.

"I'm glad to be married to you," Zorzal said softly a few minutes later. "For however long it lasts."

It took her a moment to understand what he meant. "You still think my father will come for me?"

"Don't you?"

"No," she said. She had never truly expected it; now, across a half dozen borders, it seemed unlikelier than ever.

"I'm sorry, Princess."

She didn't answer, and soon they were both asleep.

~

It was a long stretch of days before they reached the capital of Esrania—Violet tried to count, but quickly became distracted and lost track. They took a cart into the main part of the city, and as they were leaving Zorzal and the cart driver had a quick conversation in a language Violet didn't recognize—Esranian, she assumed. She knew five languages, but that was not one of them.

"He says the king is supposed to be returning to the city in the next few days; he's been travelling, searching for a bride, but no luck, I guess. We got lucky, beating him here; it's impossible to move through the city on parade days."

"King Thrushbeard," she said quietly, remembering how she had mocked him when she rejected his proposal. He had been a good, kind man, and his bushy, unkempt, uneven beard had been the closest thing she could think of to a legitimate complaint. She knew it had taken him by surprise, the rejection itself as well as the cruelty of it. They had spent some time together, in the week that he was visiting, and had got on well enough; she knew he had thought she liked him. She had liked him, just not enough to want to marry him.

The rejection had been cruel, but she was in the habit, by then, of cruelty, at least when it came to her suitors. She did not know how to push them away kindly, did not even know if it could be done. (She had tried to be kind only once, last summer, presented with a suitor who was all of fourteen years old. He had been there at his father's insistence, and had wanted the marriage no more than Violet had. He had been easy to reject, because Violet's father had not wanted the marriage either; he would not have tolerated a child groom, even had Violet taken leave of her senses enough to consider it.)

(She worried, still, about that boy—wondered if it wouldn't have been wiser, even kinder, to marry him after all, lest his father have better success marrying him to some other grown woman. As her husband, he would have been kept safe, would have been allowed to be a child.)

"Do you regret turning him down?" Zorzal asked.

"Who?"

"King Thrushbeard?"

"Oh," she said. She had still been thinking of young Robbie, far more afraid of marriage than she had been. "No, I don't regret it."

It was a few minutes before her mind caught up and she thought to ask, "How did you know who I meant, when I said King Thrushbeard?"

"It was the talk of the palace by the time I reached the back door."

"Oh."

"Don't worry; the city is large enough I'm sure you'll never encounter him again."

"I'm sure he wouldn't recognize me if I did."

They stayed in the main part of the city just long enough to buy a few days' worth of food, and then moved on toward the outskirts, toward their destination.

They came at last to what would be their home, a small building that might be called a cottage if one were feeling generous; shack or hut would be more accurate. It was small and brown and drab, with a few shuttered windows and a badly thatched roof.

The door was not locked, nor even properly latched; it swung open with a dreadful creaking sound as soon as Zorzal touched it.

The inside was a single room, dark and coated thickly in dirt and cobwebs. Zorzal went to open the shutters on one window. Violet went to another, and as soon as the latch was undone both shutters fell off and onto the ground outside.

Zorzal laughed. "It's not in the best shape."

"Really? I hadn't noticed."

When the rest of the windows were open—with no more breakages—it was light enough inside to see a small table and two mismatched chairs, a spinning wheel with a broom and a basket on the floor beside it, and what might have once been a mattress in the corner of the room. There was a small fireplace with a few rotted logs stacked beside it, and a cupboard on the wall above the table; the room was otherwise empty.

Zorzal took Violet's bag, and set it down on the table along with his own. The table wobbled as he did so—one leg was shorter than the others. Violet went and kicked at the mattress, and a few mice scurried out. There was a damp, musty smell to it.

Inside the cupboard they found two chipped bowls, two plates, two mugs, two spoons, one knife, a few scraps of cloth, and a bit of what must once have been food, but was now a great mass of mold.

Zorzal used the cloth to pick up the mold, and tossed the whole mess of it out the broken window.

"We'll go back to the city tomorrow and buy what we need," Zorzal said, "or as much of what we need as we can afford. What's most important?"

"Food," Violet said; she had learned quickly that food was always the most important thing. "We'll need—is there a water source nearby?"

"A well, I think. Behind the house. We'll have to see if it's still good. We'll have to fix the shutters, and the lock on the door. I expect the roof will leak, but we won't find the holes until it rains."

"Buckets, then. To catch the leaks so we aren't flooded when it happens."

"Firewood."

"We'll need to be sure the chimney's not blocked before we light anything," Violet said, recalling a lecture she'd once received from a palace chimney sweep.

"Oh," Zorzal said.

"I've no idea how."

"Me either," Zorzal said.

"At least the weather is warm."

He nodded. "A hammer and nails, for the repairs. The bed—I don't know what to do about the bed."

"We'd be better to sleep on the floor. It's riddled with mice and mold."

They went out to check the well; the bucket was intact, as was the mechanism to raise and lower it, and the water they brought up was clear and good. They collected the broken shutters from the ground to bring inside.

"Cooking," Violet said suddenly, as they reentered the shack. "We'll need the fireplace for cooking."

She'd never cooked before; she wasn't sure that Zorzal had either. She didn't know for how long he'd been a wandering minstrel, or what sort of life he'd led before. Odd, she thought, to still know so little of her husband; she should ask him.

It was too late in the day to go back into the city and return again, but early enough still that there was plenty of daylight left. They dragged the dreadful mattress outside, and beat it with the broom until they were sure all the mice had fled, then left it sitting on the ground in hopes that the fresh air would help it somewhat.

Back inside, they went carefully through the contents of Violet's bag for the first time since the very beginning. There were still a few pearls left, and the ruby broach. The cloak was a little ragged, but perfectly useable still. The book was fine, only slightly water-damaged around the edges. Of the three dresses she'd left the palace with, one was hopelessly damaged, essentially rags. One, she'd never even put on, and it was therefore still in perfect condition. The third was not as lovely as it had been, but the very fine material it had been made of was still usable, and it could therefore be sold to a seamstress. A few of the more delicate ribbons had been ruined, likely by the rain early on, but most were fine.

"We can sell whatever we mean to here," Zorzal said. "I grew up in the city; no one will accuse me of theft, and if they did I could defend myself."

Violet put the two better dresses, the ribbons, and the remaining pearls in a neat little stack to be taken back into the city. She hesitated over the two remaining items.

"Keep the book," Zorzal advised her. "And tell me why you chose that broach to bring with you."

"I chose it because it was the first thing I saw at the top of my jewelry box. But I—it was a gift on my fourteenth birthday, from a baron who hoped I would marry his son."

"You started that early?"

"No," she said. "No. He wasn't like the others. The son was my friend, and I would have considered the match, at least, when we were a bit older. But he died in a hunting accident a few months after that birthday."

He was quiet for a moment, and then he said, "We'll keep the broach."

"Can we afford to?"

"I am not yet destitute enough to sell off your childhood."

She nodded; he took the broach and the book and set them in the little cupboard.

~

In the city the next morning, after they had sold off all of Violet's remaining belongings, and Zorzal's little leather pouch was heavy with coins, they went shopping. First was the food, mostly grains and root vegetables, then a hammer and nails. Zorzal counted out their remaining coins carefully, and announced that they could afford a fresh bale of hay to restuff their rotten mattress. Finally, they bought a bit of soap—not enough to bathe with, but enough for washing hands and faces and dishes.

Violet's public bath, she had learned a few weeks after, had cost an entire pearl. Cleanliness was not a luxury they could often afford.

"There's a river," Zorzal offered, "near the city. People bathe in it often, but there's even less privacy than at the bath house. And it is not unusual for people like us to go some time without washing thoroughly. Perhaps in the future we can purchase a basin large enough to bathe in, and learn to make our own soap."

Violet nodded. She was more concerned, just then, with the food. A woman was selling cheese and butter; she convinced Zorzal to buy the butter.

Back at their little shack, they were faced once again with the problem of the chimney.

"Couldn't we just light it, and hope for the best?"

Violet shook her head. She'd been told in great detail about the problems with that, when she was eight or nine and had gone through a stage where she wanted to know how everything worked. She had spent several weeks trailing behind various members of palace staff and, she was sure, generally being a nuisance. But the chimney sweep she'd spent three days with had been very patient.

"All right," Zorzal said, "then I suppose you'd better get up there and take a look."

"Me?"

"You're the one who knows about chimneys."

"But it's such a small space."

"And you're smaller than I am."

"I don't actually know how to clean a chimney."

"You know more than me."

Reluctantly, Violet approached the fireplace. She wasn't sure how to go about cleaning the chimney; surely it would be too dark to see any blockages. After some consideration, she took the broom by the bristles and drove its handle up into the chimney as far as she could. She felt the handle hit something, and stepped back just before it came tumbling down; it landed with a thud, raising a cloud of ash that flew into her face.

Zorzal stepped forward, patting her on the back as she coughed. "Is that a dead raccoon?"

Violet nodded. "Good thing we checked. I'm going to wash my face; you can bury it."

When she returned to the shack, her face no longer full of ash, she could smell that the corpse had been rotting; the scent lingered, though Zorzal had taken the thing away. She opened all the windows, airing-out being the only solution she could think of for the problem, here. At home she would have sprayed perfume or lit a scented candle, or just avoided the affected room until the smell had passed. Of course, at home, a dead animal would not have been left in their chimneys for long enough to rot.

She took up the broom again, feeling rather foolish for having washed up before the task was done. Finding no more blockages with the handle, she spun the broom around and used the bristles to scrub the ashy walls of the chimney as far up as she could reach, then sent Zorzal to the roof to do the same thing from the other end. The bulk of the chimney was uncleanable, narrower than the ones in the palace, too narrow for Violet to climb up into. Zorzal lowered a rope down the chimney from his place on the roof, to be sure there were no other large blockages; when the end of the rope appeared in the fireplace, they knew there was a clear path out of the house for the smoke to follow.

"Now," Zorzal said, as they both stood again in front of the fireplace, "if only one of us knew how to cook."

"Surely, you must have had to make your own food, at some point in your travels."

He shook his head. "If I was to do my own cooking while I travelled, I would have to bring a cooking pot, a—a ladle, perhaps a—it would only have been extra luggage. Better to eat in towns when I can, and to carry lasting food when I can't."

"Well. We've the pot, now. It must go on this bar, I suppose? And we should—we should start with water."

"And what are we cooking?" Zorzal asked.

"I haven't decided yet."

"We've oats, and carrots, and potatoes. I don't suppose we could have eaten that raccoon?"

"I am not yet hungry enough to resort to eating rotten vermin with unknown cause of death."

Zorzal nodded. "I'll take the pot to the well and fill it; you can decide what to put in."

"I wonder how one makes bread," he said, later, as they ate their dinner of undercooked potatoes.

Violet shrugged. "I wonder how one affords meat."

"One kills it oneself, I suppose."

"Oh."

"We'll need more money. For traps, if we want meat. For flour, if we want bread. Herbs and spices. Blankets, cloaks, warm clothing for when winter comes, or the materials to make them. An axe, for chopping more firewood. We'll need so much more money."

He looked as dismayed as Violet felt, as their list of things to purchase steadily grew. She should have brought more of her jewelry.

"You make—do you make good money, playing? I suppose I still don't have a good sense of what things cost."

"Good enough, I think. It's always been enough before, but I haven't had a wife or a home before."

"I'll need to work too, then."

"Doing what, sweeping chimneys?"

She glanced around the room, thinking, and her eyes caught on the spinning wheel. "I'll spin," she said. "I'll make yarn."

"And have you any idea how to do that?"

"No," she admitted. "But I can sew, and embroider. Surely making yarn and thread cannot be so different from using it?"

"I wouldn't know," Zorzal said. "Tomorrow, when we go back into town, we can buy a bit of wool to try it."

~

Violet had worn wool, of course, but had never worked much with it, and had seldom worn it against her skin. Wool was for outer layers; her underthings were silk or linen. She sewed most often with silk, which was soft and fine and lovely. She had thought that, if anything, wool would be easier, being less slippery than silk.

Wool was not easier. Perhaps, she told herself, it would be, were she ever able to make it resemble embroidery floss. She could not get it near that stage.

The wool came to her in a great tangled mass, oddly oily. She took it to the spinning wheel, which she realized quickly that she had no idea how to operate. Zorzal was outside, working, she thought, on the broken shutters, which at least saved her the embarrassment of working with an audience.

It was coarse; she didn't like the feel of it running through her fingers, or the slight oily residue it left behind. She spent some time examining the wheel before she began trying to spin in earnest, but it did her little good. By the time Zorzal reentered the hut, carrying a large stack of wood which he set down near the fireplace, she had about two feet of yarn, loose in some spots, matted in others, and lumpy throughout. Her hands were red and irritated.

When she held out her poor attempt at yarn to Zorzal, he ignored it and took her hands in his instead, frowning.

"It's fine," she said. "I think the oil just irritated my skin. I'll get used to it, and I'll get better at the spinning."

"The lanolin," he said.

"What?"

He shook his head. "I'll not have you working with a material that gives you a rash."

"I'll adjust."

"I can't afford to buy as much wool as it'll take you to learn, either."

"Oh."

"We'll find something better for you to do. For now you can work on the house, and I'll go into the city and play. It won't be so hard, once the house is put back together."

The next day, they worked to fix the broken shutter; it was crooked by the time they were done, and couldn't quite latch correctly, but at least it was attached to the window again.

Violet missed glass windowpanes terribly.

For the next week or so, Zorzal took his lute into the city, and Violet stayed at home, learning to cook and clean. It shouldn't have been possible for a space this small to take this long to clean, but it had been abandoned for many years, and the filth was pervasive. She destroyed the ancestral homes of many spiders, cobwebs spreading from one end of the shack to the other. She wiped away one layer of grime on the floors to discover another, stickier layer beneath, which their bare feet caught on until she had spent hours scrubbing it.

And then it rained.

It was during daylight, at least, and at a time when Zorzal was home, and they had purchased three buckets a few days ago.

There were far more than three leaks in the roof.

Violet dragged their newly stuffed mattress, clothing, and Zorzal's lute to the driest area. With the buckets already set over the first spots where dripping began, he took the pot from the fire, then the mugs and bowls, and then the plates, to catch more water. When they were all in use, he set the spoons and knife out.

"And how much water do you think a knife will collect?" Violet asked him.

"It's to mark the spot, so I know which parts of the roof to repair."

"Do you know how to repair a roof?"

"No idea. But we didn't know how to clean a chimney either, did we?"

It was a heavy rain, but it did not last for long, and when it was over they walked carefully around the various water-catchers and water-markers scattered across the floor, it being too late at night to begin roof repairs.

In the morning they went out to examine the roof.

"It's thatched," Violet observed, thus making use of her entire knowledge of roofing.

"So I suppose we'd need more thatching?" Zorzal suggested.

"Or the money to hire someone with the faintest idea what they were doing."

Zorzal went back inside to collect their money pouch, the contents of which he dumped out onto their table. Violet didn't know how much a roofer would cost, but she strongly suspected it was more than what they had.

~

The rain had, if nothing else, finally cleared the last of the grime from the hut, which meant that Violet no longer had anything productive to do with her time. Except for cooking, but it only took so many hours each day to prepare food for two people.

Zorzal was repairing the roof, or attempting to, whenever he was home and there was daylight. His plan was to lift up bits of thatching, nail down thin strips of wood over the holes, and then lie the thatching back down. Violet wasn't sure if this was the correct way to repair a roof; neither was Zorzal.

The main difficulty with this plan was tracing the drip markers on the floor up to the outside of the roof. Zorzal's solution to that problem was to haul a bucket of water up onto the roof, pour it out where he thought there might be a hole, and have Violet, standing inside, report whether or not the water came through into the

house. He then marked each hole with a nail, planning to come back
to the actual repairs when all the holes had been located.

It was not an excellent solution.

When Violet was quite fed up with the whole process, she
convinced Zorzal to spend a day in the city, giving her a tour—she'd
only seen the parts of it relevant to their shopping, thus far.

He took her to see various chapels, and to walk around the
outer wall of the palace. There was a garden attached to the palace
that was open to the public, and they spent an hour or two walking
through it, before he took her to the market—there were a few
things they needed to buy, but it was mostly, he said, to see things.

There was a man selling the most intricate pottery she'd ever
seen, and two young girls selling garlands of pink and yellow flowers.
There were blankets and rugs and dresses, long yards of the kind of
fine, brocade fabric she would once have worn multiple times each
week. There was a glass-blower selling his wares, and they lingered
there for some time; Zorzal was fascinated, and discussed the
process with the artist in rapid Esranian. There was a woman selling
little woven baskets—charming, delicate things made of reeds. She
had them set out on a small table, and sat at a stool behind it,
working to make more. Violet watched her hands move, entranced.

When they had bought what they needed most, and stored it in
their bags, it was nearly night, and Zorzal led her not back the way
they had come, but in the opposite direction. "The sunset is
beautiful over the river," he told her, "if you do not mind walking
home in the dark."

"I do not mind."

It was a wide, winding river, which flowed slowly and lazily, and
as they walked beside it Zorzal slipped his hand into hers. The
sunset was a brilliant pink, reflected on the rippling surface of the
water, but Violet hardly saw it, focused as she was on their joined
hands. The sky faded slowly to a soft periwinkle shade, and they
reached a part of the river where reeds were growing.

Violet remembered the little baskets; she had watched the
woman work for some time, and it had not looked so hard.

"Can we pick some reeds?" she asked.

"I suppose so."

She separated her hand from his reluctantly, then slipped off her shoes, lifted her skirts, and waded into the shallow water. The reeds were harder to pick than she'd imagined, thick and slippery, but with Zorzal's help it did not take long to collect a good bundle of them, which she carried in the outermost layers of her skirt, along with her shoes and Zorzal's both, rather than put their wet feet back into them. It was a long, slow walk home beneath the darkening sky, their feet growing steadily muddier, and Violet felt warm and right.

In the morning there was Violet's best attempt at porridge, which was just slightly better than Zorzal's best, and then he was off into the city with his lute. She washed the dishes they'd used, and then went to the stack of reeds sitting on the floor.

She wanted so badly to be useful. She had spent so many years fighting against marriage, but now that it had come to her, she was determined to be an excellent wife, to prove, to prove—she wasn't sure, exactly. To prove something to someone, though she would never see anyone she knew again. To prove to herself, perhaps, that she was more than a spoilt princess causing political troubles for her father. To convince herself that she had been merely uninterested in marriage, and not horribly afraid of it. To prove that her father's betrayal had not destroyed her.

She would be useful. She would not be a burden to the husband who had not wanted her. He had already restructured his life entirely for her limitations; they had travelled across half a continent to build a home, and now he would travel no more, though he loved travel dearly. His music had been enough to feed and clothe him, and he had not needed housing. It could not feed and clothe and house them both, and so she would find a way to pull her own weight; she would not, by her ineptitude, force him to get a different, better job that he would not love.

The basket-making had not looked difficult. She was unsure what sort of money it might bring in, but certainly any money at all would be an improvement.

There was a very sharp knife in their cupboard now; Violet took it up and cut a few reeds into shorter, narrower pieces, thinking that would be an easier way to start.

Baskets were woven. It was not, she reasoned, so different from using a loom, which she had done at times. Indeed, the basket-making went much more smoothly than the spinning had. Caught up in her task, she did not notice for several minutes that the sharp edges of the reeds had cut into her palms and fingers. It was only when she noticed a streak of blood on the half-finished basket that she realized what was happening.

Her hands would adjust, she told herself firmly, using the edge of her underskirt to wipe the blood away. Her hands were soft and white, though not as white as they had been when she left home. She had seen other women's hands as they travelled—innkeepers and farmers, mostly—their hands were strong and calloused. With time, hers would be too. And the best way to speed up that process was to use them.

She ripped off the skirt edge she'd been using and wrapped both hands with it, protecting her palms, at least, from the reeds. And then she resumed her work. When the basket was done, she went to the well, and washed both the basket and her hands as thoroughly as she could.

It was not an excellent basket, lopsided, and more tightly woven in some spots than others. Still, it was better for a first attempt than her yarn had been, and it would be far easier to build her skill in this area; raw wool had to be purchased, and reeds could be plucked from the river as one pleased.

She set the basket in the center of their crooked table, and went to begin their supper. She was becoming better at cooking potatoes, and they had a bit of dried meat today, as well. Violet had asked an old woman on the street yesterday how to make bread; the woman had laughed, but told her, and they'd purchased what they needed. She was not certain she would remember the instructions. Perhaps she should have begun this morning, or even last night, when they were still fresh in her mind, but she had been excited about the prospect of basketmaking.

By the time Zorzal came home, she had a small, badly-risen loaf of bread, as well as potatoes and jerky, which she hoped she had boiled for long enough that it would cease to be jerky, and transform into a softer, more appealing meat instead. It was perhaps a vain hope; she had little experience in cooking, but thought that more time was meant to produce softer food.

"I've made a basket," she said.

"So you have," Zorzal said, sounding pleased. He poured a small stream of copper coins into it, then joined her near the fire. "I saw a man selling chickens," he said. "I thought we might consider buying a pair."

"Can we afford that?"

"Not today. But with time, perhaps."

"It would be good to have fresh eggs," Violet said, a little wistful. She'd had a poached egg for breakfast every day for years, before her father sent her away.

She set the table, and Zorzal brought the pot over from the fire, pouring food into their bowls. Violet broke the bread and offered him a piece—it looked cooked through, at least.

He caught her by the wrist, turning her hand over to study it. "What happened to your hand?"

"Nothing," she lied.

He took the bread from her and pulled her wrist closer, to better see in the low light of their hut. "It's all torn up. Show me the other one."

She did, reluctantly, and his frown deepened.

"What have you been doing?"

"It was the reeds for the basket," she admitted, "but it's only because I have princess hands; they'll be stronger with time."

"Perhaps they will be, but you shan't be cutting yourself up in the meantime."

She pulled her hands away. "The basket's so much better than the yarn, though; with a bit more practice I could sell them."

"I'll not have you hurt yourself," he said.

"I want to be useful. I want to do something worth doing, something that contributes to this household."

"There'll be time enough for that," he said softly. He reached across the table to take her hands again. "Violet. I'll not have you hurt. You'll cook, and I'll sing, and we'll make do until something better comes along."

"I'm no good at cooking, either."

"Better than me," he said. He released her hands, and took the bit of bread she'd dropped.

"It's good," he reported after a moment. Violet tasted her own bit, and disagreed—it was nearly tasteless. The potatoes were fine, at least, though the meat had not become good and tender as she was hoping.

"It will be all right, Princess. It takes time, building a whole new life."

~

She made bread and bread until she was content with the results, which meant many weeks of eating bread that was decidedly questionable. Zorzal did not complain. He went into the city with his lute often, and when he was home, spent most of his time working slowly and carefully on the roof. Fortunately it did not often rain here.

He earned enough money to buy her herbs and spices, and she learned which ones she needed. Her porridges and stews improved steadily, as well as her breads, and at night before bed, Zorzal would play and sing for her, or she would read something from her book.

They had fallen into a comfortable routine, and Violet was very nearly happy. She thought seldom of her father, and slept comfortably each night with her husband, on their lumpy straw mattress on the floor.

~

One day, while Zorzal was in the city, and there was nothing much to do in the house, Violet leaned against the back wall, and fell right through.

She scrambled hastily to her feet, looking with dismay at the hole she'd just created in the side of their house.

The wood was rotten; she didn't know how they'd failed to notice before. It must have been the first time they'd put any weight on that area.

She didn't—it was bad enough, having to patch up a dozen holes in the roof, and now a wall—the rot covered at least half the length of the wall, and to repair it—the cost of new wood alone, and the hours they would have to spend on it, hours Zorzal wouldn't be able to spend earning money—she was crying when he found her.

"Oh," he said, seeing the hole in the wall. "That isn't good."

Then he turned away from the wall, and knelt down in front of her, sitting in the dirt in tears. He took her hands. "Your dress is ripped. Are you hurt?"

She shook her head. "Small bruises. Maybe splinters."

He released her hands to cup her face instead. "It will be all right, Princess. It's only a wall."

And he kissed her.

He stood up a moment later, as if nothing had happened, and pulled her to her feet as well. "Come on, you'd best get changed so we can mend that skirt. I'll see how far the rot goes."

She was sitting by the fire, stitching up the tear in her skirt, when he reentered the house, stepping right through the hole instead of going around to the door.

"Surely building a wall cannot be so hard," he said, though he did not sound particularly confident.

"We can sell my broach to afford the wood."

"No," he said. "We'll manage. I might—I might be able to call in a favor. I have an old friend who is not unskilled in carpentry. He could help with the roof as well, perhaps. I should—I should have thought to ask him sooner."

He kissed her again before going to bed, again like it was nothing at all, though only on the cheek this time. He fell asleep quickly, as he usually did, while she lay awake for long hours, whole new worlds opening up to her. She hadn't thought—she hadn't allowed herself to think—

She had never wanted anything in her life so much as she wanted, in this moment, a full, thorough bath in warm water. It had been so long since she had bathed, she had stopped noticing the smell, and had not thought of it in many weeks. But now—

She wanted to have soft, clean skin for Zorzal to kiss. She wanted—she wanted to be kissed.

There had not been a kiss to seal their marriage; she had not missed it at the time. She had never wanted to be kissed, had not been kissed since she was a small child, by her nursemaid and by her father.

It still hurt, thinking of her father. She mostly tried not to.

It was much more pleasant to think of Zorzal. To think of her husband.

He would not be any cleaner to kiss than she was, she supposed; why should one dirty person mind kissing another?

Still, it would be good to have a bath.

She woke before him, though she had fallen asleep long after, and was sitting beside him as his eyes opened.

"Zorzal," she said.

"Violet."

She leaned forward and kissed him, carefully; he kissed her back before standing.

"I'll need to find my friend; I'll be back in a bit."

She sat there as the door swung closed behind him. Apparently, kissing was a thing they were doing now, and apparently, they weren't going to talk about it.

"My friend will come tomorrow," he reported when he came home an hour later. "Would you like to hear something magnificent?"

"All right."

"According to my friend, who recently helped repair the roof of the palace stable, the whole court has taken to calling our king King Thrushbeard."

"Really?"

"The entire kingdom has long agreed that it is a truly terrible beard. Just exactly like a bird's nest." He pulled a silver coin from his pocket and handed it to her. "Here, in case you've forgotten what it looks like. Though my friend says the coin doesn't do it justice."

She looked at the coin, at the tiny face of the man (of one of the many men) who could have been her husband. His other features were mostly obscured by the beard. She handed it back to him; she had more pressing concerns than King Thrushbeard's beard.

"'Zorzal," she said. "Zorzal, are we—are we to be married?"

"Well, I thought—I thought perhaps we could be a little married, and not face the eventual wrath of your father."

"A little married," Violet agreed, though she doubted her father would ever know. She only wanted to kiss her husband.

~

In the morning Zorzal's friend arrived. He was a tall man with a large smile, who got down immediately to the work of repairing the wall. He'd brought with him a cart full of supplies, pulled by two mules; Violet had not been near any animals but mice since they'd finished their journey, and spent much time petting their velvety noses and feeding them bits of carrot she really couldn't spare.

She had intended to help with the repairs, as much as she could, but Zorzal's friend told her that the mules didn't like the sounds of construction, the hammering and sawing and general banging around, and she would be most helpful if she took them both a good distance away for a few hours.

She did, first collecting her book and Zorzal's spare pair of pants, which needed mending. She walked the mules a half hour or so out from home, in the opposite direction from the city, and let them graze while she mended and read. It was a beautiful, sunny day, and she had Zorzal's hat, which she had not worn much since reaching the hut, and which she had missed. It felt like a part of him, and wearing it she felt they were linked. A little married, he'd said last night. She thought she would like being a little married.

When she returned with the mules, the wall was done, and they set her to work passing supplies up to them, both standing on the roof. The day passed quickly, and Zorzal's friend left shortly before dark. Violet realized as the cart was driving away that she had never learned his name.

~

Being a little married meant quick kisses and joined hands and the lifting of a tension Violet had hardly noticed until it was gone.

When it rained again the roof held, and they sat pressed together in their bed, listening as it hit the roof.

Their days fell into a happy, easy pattern, and Zorzal stayed home with her for many days, the two of them venturing out only once when they were in need of more food.

But too soon the money dried up, and Zorzal took his lute back into the city, and Violet was back to spending long hours in the hut alone.

~

"Are you still determined to have a job?" Zorzal asked her one evening when he had come home. They had discussed it many times now, and never got anywhere.

"I am."

"How do you think selling would suit you?"

"Selling what?"

"I spoke to a potter this morning. She makes beautiful work, and she's looking for someone to take it to market for her, so she doesn't have to take time away from making it."

"I could sell pottery," Violet said. She'd never sold anything before, but certainly it would be better than the career paths she'd tried already. There was no need to create anything herself, only to convince other people that they must own the beautiful things already created.

Zorzal took her the next day to meet the potter, who was a large, cheerful woman old enough to be Violet's grandmother. She came forward to embrace Zorzal as he came through the door. "My little songbird," she said. "Months and months and months it's been since you've visited me, and now I get you twice in two days!"

Zorzal ducked his head, embarrassed. "I'm sorry, Auntie. But see, I've brought you my wife, just as I said I would. This is Violet, and Vi, this is my Auntie Inez, a dear friend of my mother's."

The woman hugged Violet as well, and then took them both around her studio, showing them a few finished pots, but mostly pots in progress. There were pots she was in the middle of painting, and pots half-formed with the clay still soft and cool. She showed

160

Violet the wheel she used to build the pots, and the fire, hotter-than-hot, that she used to bake them.

When the tour was over, she loaded a large crate with pottery, loaded the crate into a small cart, and directed them to the marketplace.

"You could have told me in advance," Violet said as they pulled the crate to the market, "that Inez was a dear friend you've known since childhood, and not some stranger you met on the street and offered my services to. You made it sound last night as if you'd just first met her yesterday."

"Does it matter?" Zorzal asked.

"A bit. I've never met anyone you knew—anyone you cared about—before. Well, the carpenter, but we weren't even introduced. It would have been nice to know what to expect. Meeting the best friend of your husband's dead mother is nothing at all like meeting a stranger."

"I'll tell you if we're ever in this situation again. Here, this looks like the place she said. Do you want me to stay?"

"Will you make good money here?"

"I do better a few blocks over."

"Go on, then. I'll manage."

Selling the pottery was easy. It was beautiful, functional work, and Violet thought it was priced quite fairly, though admittedly she still struggled to understand how much money was worth, especially as they had passed through multiple countries, with multiple currencies.

At the end of each day, she took the crate and its remaining contents back to Inez, and she picked them up again each morning. It took her a week to sell the first crate, and three days to sell the second. It was on her second day with the third crate that disaster struck.

It struck in the form of a large, redheaded man in fine brocade, paler than was typical in this part of the world, nearly as pale as Violet had been at the beginning of their journey. He rode a large bay stallion, which was wild and afraid; he clearly had poor control over the animal, and when he came close enough for the strong scent to reach her, Violet realized it was because he was drunk.

It was all she could do, as the horse bore down on her little rug covered in pottery, to scramble out of the way. Carla, selling fruit a few feet away, did the same, and Beto, who'd made the rug Violet was using, barely had time to pull his small son out from beneath the horse's hooves.

The man dismounted a few feet away, laughing, and stumbled away on foot, leading the horse.

The few of them who'd had the near miss huddled together, examining the damage. Beto's son was crying, and several of his rugs were dirtied and torn. Carla's fruit was all crushed, and Violet's pots all shattered.

"It was Lord Ferdinand," Carla told her. "He's the king's cousin. The only noble we all recognize on sight, and only because of—because of things like this."

"Drunken lout," Beto muttered. "He'll never pay us back for the damages."

"Of course not," Carla agreed. "Why would someone as powerful as him spare a thought for our livelihoods?" She picked up one of the least-bruised pieces of fruit and offered it to Beto's son, still crying. "Here, sweetheart, it's all right. He's gone now."

When Zorzal arrived to check on her, as he often did at midday, she had loaded most of the pottery shards back into the crate. She, Carla, and Beto were eating the fruit too damaged to sell but still good enough to eat, and Beto's little boy had recovered from the experience and was toddling between them. Carla offered Zorzal a peach.

"It was Lord Ferdinand," she told him. "Vi's whole stock was destroyed."

"I'm sorry," Violet said, though she knew it was not her fault, and Zorzal shook his head, and took her in his arms.

They sat together on the ground for a few minutes, sharing the peach as Carla told him the story. And then they had to take the crate back to Inez.

Zorzal told her they would pay, of course, for the pottery that had been broken. She named a price, reluctantly, after he had insisted several times. Violet stood back silently throughout the conversation. She knew offering to pay was the right thing to do, and would have felt bad if they hadn't. But it was so much money.

There was no talk of taking another crate to market the next day. Violet stayed at home, again, while Zorzal went into the city to play and sing. With nothing else to do, she threw herself again into cooking, experimenting when she could, though never too outrageously, as they could not afford to waste food, and all the experiments must be eaten.

"You're becoming a wonderful cook," Zorzal told her one night.

"There's nothing much else I can do."

"It wasn't your fault, what happened with the pottery. He was a drunken lout rich enough to do whatever he wants. And we've almost paid it back."

"Only because Inez was so kind. She must have undercharged."

He shrugged. "Her kindness does not change the fact it was not your fault." He stood, bending down to kiss her cheek as he walked past. "I'll ask around in the city tomorrow. See if I can find something for you."

"Good." Things had been hard—things had been hard since they were married, truly, but harder still since the pottery had broken, and most of Zorzal's earnings had gone into repaying it.

They fell asleep kissing that night, and when she woke he had already left for the morning.

~

"There's a job opening for a kitchen maid," Zorzal told her as he peeled an onion that night. "In the palace."

"The palace," Violet repeated.

He nodded. "You don't have to."

"It sounds like a good job."

"It is. But we'll get by without it. Something else will come along."

"I can work in the palace," Violet said. After all, it wasn't her palace. It was the palace of a suitor she'd rejected, but to be fair, every palace on the continent, and quite a few elsewhere, was the palace of a suitor she'd rejected. King Thrushbeard had been long ago, and she doubted they would recognize each other now, should a king and a kitchen maid somehow meet. There would be no one else in the palace to recognize her, to remember her former station and cause embarrassment.

"If you're sure."

"I'm sure," she said.

"I'll make the arrangements tomorrow, and you can start the next day." He'd finished peeling and chopping the onion; he took it to the pot on the fire, dropping a kiss on her head as he passed.

That night, she leaned over to kiss him as they lay next to each other in bed. He pulled back, kissed her forehead, and rolled over, away from her.

"Zorzal—"

"Go to sleep, Violet."

~

She loved working in the kitchens. Cooking and chopping ingredients and washing dishes were all things she knew how to do already, and she liked being told exactly what to do, rather than fumbling around trying to work it out for herself. It was good to be busy, good to walk into the city each morning with Zorzal, and back to their home each night.

At home, most of her energy went into her new goal—she and Zorzal had been officially married for nearly a year, and "a little married" for several weeks. She thought it was past time to transition into a full marriage.

Zorzal was not cooperating.

It wasn't—she didn't want to pressure him into something he didn't want. But she was certain that he did want it; she knew him so well, by now, and their lives were so thoroughly entwined. Every time he pulled away from her he did it more reluctantly than the time before. But every time he still pulled away.

Her job did not pay very well, she thought, but it paid well enough for her. Having two steady incomes instead of one was wonderful, no matter how small each income was. Zorzal began talking again of chickens, but they would first need to build a chicken coop, and so their spare money was being saved now for that.

~

One day when Violet was not working, Zorzal went into the city without her, and came home not long after with cheese and eggs and two small cakes.

"It's our anniversary," he told her when she met him at the door.

She took her cake, and stood on her toes to kiss him. She'd had no idea—she could hardly believe a year had passed. "Then perhaps it's time we finished getting married," she suggested, and he took a step back, shaking his head.

"I love you, Zorzal. Don't you love me?"

"Of course I do. You know I do."

"Then why can't we have this? I want this, you want this, we've been married for months—for a year."

"You know why. Your father—"

"Isn't here. Isn't coming. Clearly doesn't care at all what I do, or he wouldn't have—I love you. I want you. Let me be your wife in more than name. Please."

He kissed her, then, sudden and hard, and she fumbled behind her back for the door handle, determined to reach the bed—their bed—before he changed his mind.

"Violet," he said. "Violet, I don't—"

"I love you," she said again. "Zorzal."

He stepped back abruptly. "We can't."

"Why?"

"You're the princess," he said, as if that meant anything anymore, and kissed her again, on the cheek this time, before going back outside.

They didn't talk the rest of the day, not as she cooked the eggs, nor as they ate their eggs and cheese and cake, nor as they prepared for bed. In the morning Zorzal walked her to work, as he always did,

165

and while she worked, Violet planned out how she would make her next argument.

She waited to begin it until they were home, sitting across from each other at their little table, finishing up with dinner.

"If you truly believe my father will come for me, after all this time—if you truly believe that, then that's why—we have to—an unconsummated marriage is easily annulled, Zorzal. If we—if you— then he can never take me away from you."

"He's a king, Violet. He can do whatever he wants."

"I know you want this," she said softly. "So what are you afraid of, really? It can't be just my father, not after all this time."

"This is a big step. It can't be taken back or undone. And I'm afraid that someday you'll regret it."

Violet reached across the table to take his hands. "There is nothing in the world that could ever make me regret a moment I've spent with you."

"Nothing?"

"Nothing," she promised.

He stood and let go of her hands, and she was sure he was going to walk away again. But instead he came around the table and bent to kiss her, taking her hands again and drawing her to her feet.

"I love you," he said. "Violet, I love you so much."

She woke early the next morning. Zorzal was solid and warm in the bed beside her, one arm draped around her waist. He was still asleep; she pressed a kiss to his jawline, then set her head in the space between his neck and shoulder and went back to sleep.

They woke again just in time to get dressed and rush into the city, jogging nearly the entire way to the palace, where Zorzal dropped her off. There had been no time for breakfast, and their dishes from last night were still sitting dirty on the table.

It was the most wonderful day.

Work was busy then; the king—King Thrushbeard—was getting married in a week, and there were dozens of things to be planned and prepared.

The next few days were overwhelmingly chaotic at the palace, and deliriously happy at home. She could hardly catch her breath, but it was a wonderful, floating feeling.

She was to work late the day of the king's wedding; the whole palace was. That morning when he dropped her at the back door, Zorzal pressed her against the wall and kissed her, long and slow.

"I'll be home in a few hours," she assured him, though the planned twelve to fourteen was, admittedly, more than a few.

"Too many hours," he countered, and kissed her again. Violet laughed.

"Love you, Princess," he whispered into her hair, and then he left her, lute swinging on his back as he walked away.

~

She was working furiously from the moment she walked through the door; a king's wedding feast was a major affair. She was wearing her dress with the massive pockets, which she'd extended using fabric scraps, and occasionally she would swipe a bit of food from the trays going upstairs and drop it in. There were a dozen delicacies she'd not seen since leaving her own palace, delicacies Zorzal had likely never seen at all, wonderful things she wanted to share with her wonderful husband.

When one of the head chefs called her from across the room, she thought she had been caught, but it was worse.

"I need you to take this platter upstairs."

She shook her head. "I can't—I work in the kitchen, not upstairs."

"And now I need you to take something upstairs from the kitchen."

"I—" The ballroom would be full of people she'd encountered in her old life, come from all across the continent for the wedding.

"Go on," the chef said, a little more gently. "They're just people like us, Violet. Nothing to be afraid of."

With no other choice, she took the platter and went upstairs, where she ran directly into her father almost immediately.

He caught her by the shoulders, frowning. "Violet. What on earth are you wearing?"

Her temper, dormant for the better part of a year, flared abruptly. "What am I wearing? What am I wearing? Father, you—"

She was interrupted by a hand on her shoulder, and a vaguely familiar voice asking her to dance.

She wasn't sure who the voice belonged to, but was quite certain she didn't want to find out.

"Come on," he said, "you can't say no to me on my wedding day."

King Thrushbeard.

"I couldn't say no to a king on any day," she said, turning around reluctantly.

She kept her eyes fixed firmly on their feet, reasoning that if he never saw her face there was no chance of his recognizing her. They made their way halfway through the dance before he spoke, and his voice was different now, different and so much more familiar.

"Violet," he said softly, "look at me," and she looked up into the face of her husband.

She took one stumbling step backward and froze, staring at him. The dancing continued around them, until someone crashed into her, and her pockets burst, spilling food onto the floor, and then all the dancing stopped abruptly, and all eyes were on her.

The man who'd bumped into her laughed.

It was—she recognized him, too. The man who'd destroyed her pots. Lord Ferdinand. Zor—the king was yelling at him in Esranian; she didn't know what he was saying, and she didn't care. She had to—she had to get away.

She wanted—she wanted to go home. But she didn't have a home. Her home was a lie, a trick played on her by a man angry at rejection. She wasn't—she didn't—there was only one thing to do.

She pushed her way through the crowd to her father. She was too angry at Zor—at the king, now, to bother being angry at him, too. She was crying, she thought, or had been, or was about to be, and she was dressed in filthy rags, and all she could think was that her father had loved her, once, and Zorzal never had. She couldn't even remember his real name.

"Will you take me home?"

He drew her into his arms immediately. "Come up to my rooms. I'll send for someone to prepare the carriage."

"I brought a few trunks of your things," he said when they were safely upstairs. "I was surprised you hadn't sent for them yet, but I'm beginning to think something went very wrong. Violet, what's happened?"

"What's happened?" She laughed, unamused. "You married me to a beggar. How was I to send for my things? Where did you think I would be keeping them? What use could I have for them, living like this?"

He frowned. "I married you to a king, Violet. It was—I'll admit it was a cruel trick to play, but I needed you married, and it seemed he was still willing; I never imagined the deception would last more than a few hours. You never recognized him? You've been living like a pauper, all these months, while I waited for the official announcement of your wedding?"

She shook her head. "I never—stupid of me, all he did was shave, and I never noticed, but then I only ever paid enough attention to suitors to find a reason to reject them. We've lived in a hut at the edge of the city, I've—I thought—I thought I loved him. And we were—you won't be able to marry me again. I'm sorry."

"You've nothing to be sorry for. Don't worry about any of that now. I have most of your clothing here; change into something you like and lie down a while. I'll wake you when the carriage is ready."

She chose an outfit far too nice for a long carriage ride, just because she could—her finest silk underthings and a beautiful gown with silver brocade—but had not yet started to change when there was a knock on the door.

Her father had stepped into the next room, to give her privacy for changing and to arrange for their unplanned departure, and she was alone; she went to open the door.

It was him, of course. Her husband.

"Violet," he said. "Violet, I'm sorry. I didn't mean—"

"Didn't mean what? To trick me into marrying you? To lie to me for a year? To force me to live needlessly in poverty? To embarrass me in front of your entire court and guests from every royal family in five hundred miles?"

"Vi," he said softly, and she realized that she was yelling, that she was a scullery maid yelling at a king in a wing of the palace she had no business being in.

Well, what did it matter, if his other guests saw him being yelled at by a scullery maid? What did she care for his reputation?

She cared for her father's, though, and there would doubtless be rumors about why he had a scullery maid in his chambers in the first place.

"Come inside," she said, and he did.

"Violet," he said, and she struggled to remember details of the king she'd first met, who she'd not thought of in months. That beard, that dreadful beard, and colorful, horribly unstylish clothing. Was that why he'd been such a strangely drab minstrel? For contrast? What else was there? He'd been a better candidate than many, but she had wanted none, and had paid so little attention. His voice. His awkward, stilted speech. And the accent. The accent was different.

"Violet," he said again, proving it. He said it as Zorzal had always said it, stretched out and musical. He hadn't said her name that way before; she would have recognized him if he had.

"Your accent. You didn't say my name like that, before."

"Oh, that." He shrugged. "The hut was my mother's, before she married the king. And because she wasn't noble, I grew up with an...undesirable accent. It takes a lot of effort, pronouncing things the way I'm expected to when I'm doing things like visiting other nobility."

"So. That's one thing that was real. One real thing. The accent you used to tell all your lies."

"The hut, too. My mother."

She shook her head. "Why did you do it? Do you hate me so much?"

"I don't hate you. I could never hate you."

"Then how could you play such a trick on me? How could you lie to me for so long?"

"I didn't mean to—you told me. Do you even remember that? If you paid so little attention to me that the only disguise I needed was a shave—you told me that if you didn't choose a suitor this time, your father would marry you to the next beggar that came to the door."

"I didn't think he meant it!"

"I didn't either. It wasn't a trick, it was a—it was a joke. I thought—but then he actually did it, and I didn't say anything because I was terrified of what could have—I thought better to take you with me than leave you there to be married to who knows what kind of—better that you were safe, even if it was with a man you didn't want."

"He's just told me. He married us because he recognized you."

"That's why, then—I really did think he'd regret it and come looking for you. That's why I kept the secret, to start; I thought he'd come and get you, and then perhaps you'd agree to marry me after all, if no one else would have you after our little adventure, and someday I could tell you the truth and we could laugh about it."

"I'm not laughing."

"It was a mistake. Violet, I'd—I'd liked the idea of marrying you, and you'd seemed agreeable, until the moment you rejected me in front of your whole court, and I was hurt, and maybe a little malicious for it at first, even as badly as I felt about the mess with your father, but I fell in love with you while we were travelling, and you were falling in love with me—with Zorzal, not a king, and I was afraid to ruin everything by telling you."

"And you thought that somehow everything would be fine if you never did? You could spend the next fifty years dropping me off in the kitchens and going upstairs to rule your kingdom?"

"I thought your father would catch up with us, and we'd have it all out, and maybe you wouldn't be so angry with me then, because I'd lied to you, but at least I hadn't abandoned you like he had. And then he didn't come, and didn't come, and every day it was a worse mess of lies I didn't know how to untangle, and finally I—the wedding, I thought—I thought I could frame it like a fun surprise, instead of a huge secret I'd been keeping, and then it all went wrong." He paused. "Damn Ferdinand. And the mess—I didn't think you'd be smuggling food home for us. That was—that was sweet."

"There were so many foods I didn't think you'd have been able to try before. I wanted—" She stopped suddenly, remembering that she was angry, that he was a liar hosting the party that served the foods he should never have had a chance to try.

"I love you, Violet."

"How can I believe that? How can I ever believe another word you say?"

"How could you not believe me? How could you doubt that I love you, after all the things we've shared?"

"I can doubt you because while I worked in the scullery, you were upstairs dressed in velvets. Because you were—because we— Zor—you waited until a week before this charade to consummate the marriage. How can you possibly say that wasn't a way to chain me to you in anticipation of this exact fight?"

"You spent weeks pushing for that consummation."

"And you spent weeks pretending you were afraid of my father, instead of lying about everything you were."

"I put you off and put you off, until you said nothing could make you stop loving me."

"And you knew—you knew—you couldn't have put me off for one more week? It doesn't matter that my father is taking me back; no one else will ever marry me as long as you're alive."

"And when have you ever wanted to be married? You're known on three continents for turning down every suitor you've ever met."

"That doesn't matter. That's not the point. You lied to me. That consummation was under false pretenses, and you know it. All you had to do was say no for a few more days."

"Have you stopped loving me?"

"Loving you and being able to forgive you for months of deceit are two entirely different matters."

He nodded slowly. "Don't leave. Violet, please. Take your own chambers on the opposite side of the palace if you like, only see me for court events, but stay. Please. I never meant—I'm so sorry. I didn't mean to hurt you. Please don't leave."

"I'm not remarrying you tonight."

"I know. I know, that was—that was stupid. I'm sorry."

"My father is willing to take me home. There would be no more suitors. Perhaps in a few years I could marry one of my cousins, if I marry at all. I could go back to my old life, and pretend none of these last few months happened, and never think of you again. To live the rest of my life like I did before the first suitors came—it's exactly what I've always wanted." She wondered where her father was; they were not being quiet, and it could not take this long to arrange a carriage. He must be giving them privacy.

"All right," he said quietly. "All right, Violet."

They stood there in silence for a moment, Violet unsure what else there was to say, but unready to send him away.

"Why Zorzal?" she asked. "For your name. Why did you choose that?"

"It means thrush. It also happens to be my mother's childhood pet name for me, which I thought—I thought it was a nice coincidence. And it does sound nicer than my real name, doesn't it?"

"It does," she agreed, not currently willing to admit she didn't remember his given name.

"You were happy," he said, "weren't you? In our little hut?"

"It has been the happiest time of my life."

"If you wanted me to—if it would make you stay—I could give up the crown, and we could go back. We could go home. We could pretend today never happened."

It was more tempting than it should be. "And who would rule your kingdom?" she asked.

"A cousin, I suppose. I'm not sure exactly which one is next in line."

"You don't even know who it is, and you'll put the whole kingdom in his hands?"

"What does it matter? He'll be king, now or years from now; I can't marry again any more than you can, and there will be no heirs."

"You're a man. You could marry again if you liked."

"I wouldn't. Even if we have it annulled I wouldn't. You're my wife."

"If I have a duty to my kingdom, to marry and create alliances, you certainly have a duty to produce an heir."

"I don't care. I won't—we'll annul it, if you like. But you are my wife. No one else will ever be."

Violet sighed, running a hand through her hair—it was greasy; he was perfectly clean, of course. How many days had he come home too clean, and she had somehow failed to notice? Or had he gone to the trouble of dirtying himself again before coming home?

"Here is what we will do," she said. "You will go downstairs and make your excuses to the wedding guests. I will take a long, hot bath, put on a silk nightgown, and sleep on a feather bed in a room adjoining my father's. In the morning you and I will go back to our little hut, and I will collect whatever I want to take home with me, and you will have that time, until we come back here, to change my mind."

He nodded. "Thank you, Violet." He leaned forward as if he would kiss her, but remembered himself at the last moment and pulled back.

Her father came back into the room as soon as Zorzal had gone.

"Let's prepare that bath, then," he said; she wasn't surprised that he'd been eavesdropping.

"I missed you," she told him. "I missed you so much."

He pulled her close as she started to cry, and waited until she was finished to go arrange her bath.

~

Zorzal—well, not Zorzal, but he came in the morning, in the clothes she was accustomed to seeing him in. She was dressed much more finely, the dress she'd worn into the palace yesterday being newly ripped and covered in food stains.

Violet didn't know her way around the palace, outside of the kitchens (the kitchens—she'd never gone back last night, she would be in—

It didn't matter if she would be in trouble; she would never go down into the kitchens again. She was going home today.)

174

She didn't know her way around the palace, but suspected him of taking a more circuitous route than strictly necessary, to lengthen their time together. It struck her as very unlikely that the most direct path from her father's suite to the outside ran through the portrait hall, for example.

He wasn't making much use of the extra time he'd won with her, wasn't trying to talk much. But that was not an altogether unsuccessful strategy; they had shared many hours of comfortable silence over this last year, and walking quietly beside him, she found herself forgetting that she was angry. She paused by the last portrait in the hall, the one of him, from before he'd shaved.

"It really was an awful beard," she said.

"I know. It was my cousin's idea; it seemed like a good suggestion at the time, though now I wonder if it was meant to be a joke at my expense. I've been king since I was fifteen, and sometimes my councilors struggle to remember I'm an adult now. He said it would make me look more mature. Of course, my cousin is also my valet, and clean shaven, and neither of us could be bothered with learning how to care for a beard."

Violet looked from his smiling face to the portrait. "You don't look so different, really," she said, and all the fine feeling between them evaporated.

"You didn't even see me. A shave and a stronger accent, that's all it took."

"Oh, and you saw me so clearly, did you?"

"No," he admitted. "I saw a spoilt, petty princess who didn't deserve the fate that awaited her, if her father wasn't bluffing. And I was right, wasn't I? I'd have played a song and gone on my way, if he hadn't followed through."

"He only followed through because he recognized you. If you hadn't come at all, he'd have got over his anger in a few months, and everything would have been fine."

"And I was supposed to know that? To trust his intentions, when all I knew of him was the threat I'd heard him make? I should have risked that, risked you being tied to a man who would rape you or abandon you in an alley, or God knows what?"

"You should have told me the truth as soon as we were out of the palace."

"I should have," he acknowledged. "I—I panicked. I had given my retinue a time to—to wait, for me to come back, or they were to leave without me. But I'd forgotten it, with everything that happened. I was so angry at your father, for what he'd done to you, for what he'd done to the man he thought I was. And, and at you— you had been dreadful, Violet, and I was feeling a bit—a bit spiteful, perhaps. Right up until I saw you cry yourself to sleep, and I—it was too late, my retinue was already gone, and I—I hadn't thought that through, really. And it didn't seem to matter whether you knew the truth or not, when regardless we would have to either make our own way across the continent or throw ourselves upon your father's mercy. I knew I wouldn't be living like a king anytime soon. And Vi, I was terrified the entire time. I had no idea what I was doing. I didn't spare a thought for how to break the truth to you when I was trying to make sure we both survived the journey, and by the time I felt we had room to breathe, I realized it was far too late to tell you without ruining everything."

They left the palace, making the familiar walk from there to the hut in silence. Zorzal didn't try to speak again until their rooftop— the rooftop they'd repaired—was in sight.

"Violet. I—I need you to know. I went to the palace only when I had business to attend to, and I bathed and dressed only as was necessary for that business. I didn't linger in my chambers. I didn't eat when you were going hungry. I took no money from the treasury."

"But you could have, whenever you liked. You had that option, and I did not."

"You told me you were happier than you had ever been as a princess."

"Because I was with you. I would have been happy anywhere with you. Or with the person I thought you were at this time yesterday."

She hurried ahead; he was still jogging to catch up to her when she opened the door.

Violet looked around their hut, suddenly at a loss. She'd left her whole life behind once already. She thought of the few things she'd packed and the many she'd left behind, and realized she'd never missed most of them. She'd missed the living things. Mostly the people, of course. But the horses, the hunting hounds, the cats that roamed the halls catching mice.

What would she take away from this life? The crooked basket she'd bled for? The chipped pottery? The broom, or the badly spun yarn?

(She would take her book and her broach. And the food—they didn't need it, but they couldn't leave it here to rot; someone could make use of it.)

She'd missed the people, she thought, and she turned to face her husband, standing in the open door.

"The only thing here worth keeping is you."

"Then you'll stay?"

"I'll stay." She was still angry, and thought she would be for some time. But Zorzal—she had lost so many people, this last year, and she knew she would miss Zorzal more than she'd missed all of them combined. There would be time—there would be the rest of their lives to apologize and make up and get to know each other with no lies between them.

"I'll stay," she said again, and she did not kiss him—she was not ready yet for that—but she took his hands in hers, and they walked away together.

"The Girl with No Heart in Her Body" is an original fairy tale.

"The Ogre Bride" is a mostly original story inspired by a great many fairy tales which I had not read in years at the time I wrote it, and which I remembered only in scattered fragments. These include, among others, Basile's "The Dove" (Italian), the Grimms' "The Two Kings' Children" (German), the Grimms' "The Queen Bee" (German), and Georg von Gaal's "The Grateful Beasts" (Hungarian). The male lead is named after the title character in the Grimm brothers' "Sweetheart Roland" (German). Susan's brother Thunder comes from "The Golden Root," from Giambattista Basile's *Il Pentamerone* (Italian).

"The Shoemaker Prince" is largely an original story. It was initially inspired by Schonwerth's "The Enchanted Trunk" (Bavarian), though it went off quickly in its own direction; remaining elements from the inspiration are a cobbler prince with red shoes, and a princess in a tower.

"The Man Who Forgot How to Love" is based on the ending of the Scottish story "The Daughter of the King Under Waves."

"Windows" is based on "Beauty and the Beast," written originally by Gabrielle-Suzanne Barbot de Villeneuve (French), and later by a great many other people.

"The Frog Who Married a Prince" is based on the German "Puddocky" and the Russian "The Frog Princess."

"The Princess Who Refused to Marry a Merman" is mostly an original story, though the beginning is based on "An Impossible Enchantment," by Comte de Caylus (French), and the rest of the story takes some inspiration from "The Blue Bird," by Madame d'Aulnoy (French), and from a Jewish folk tale.

"The Foolish Princess and the Wise Prince" is based on Charles Perrault's version of "Riquet with the Tuft" (French).

"Flash" is based on the Greek myth of Medusa.

"The Man with the Silver Nose" is based on the Bluebeard story type; the silver nose detail comes from an Italian version called "How the Devil Married Three Sisters."

"The Kiss and the Frog" is based on the Grimm brothers' "The Frog King, or Iron Henry" (German).

"King Lindorm" is a translation, not a retelling, of a Danish fairy tale first recorded by Svend Grundtvig, in a book entitled *Gamle Dansk Minder i Folkemunde*. It can also be found in my novel *Lindworm*.

"The Tailor and the Queen" is an original story, though it does make a brief reference to Hans Christian Andersen's "The Emperor's New Clothes" (Danish).

"Dreams Remembered" is based on the same stories as the ones that inspired "The Ogre Bride."

"The Marquis of Carabas" is based on Charles Perrault's "Puss in Boots" (French).

"Violet and Zorzal" is based on the Grimm brothers' story "King Thrushbeard" (German).

Acknowledgements

Thank you to my patrons, Jeff and Sue Prater. Lynn and Lowell Nystrom, Beth and Steve Cragle, Jamie Krause, and Sam Medlock. Thank you also to the various professors and classmates, too many to list by name, who have helped with revisions on various stories included here over the past several years.

Author's Note

This is the second edition of *The Shoemaker Prince*. Since the first edition, we have reformatted the work, corrected a few spelling mistakes, and added three new stories. The formatting changes reduced the page count significantly, so you will find that our second edition is a slightly smaller book than the first. However, this edition does contain more content. The stories "Flash," "King Lindorm," and "Dreams Remembered" are all new additions. "King Lindorm" was previously published in my first novel, *Lindworm*. For the second edition of *The Shoemaker Prince*, we have also updated the paper type for the pages of the book.